Candie Caine: A Moment of Clarity

By

Jontu

Text LEOSULLIVAN
to 22828 to join our
mailing list!

To submit a manuscript for our review,
email us at leosullivanpresents@gmail.com

Chapter 1: Candie

"Now why the hell would he do this to me of all days?" I yelled out in frustration as I threw my phone across the bathroom. Sitting down on the toilet, I placed my head in my hands as I allowed the wave of nausea to pass. I had to sit and reflect on my life. Dealing with Caine for the past four years, I still woke up every day and wondered what in the world I was doing here. I had been waiting for Caine, my boyfriend, all morning and he had yet to show his face. He hadn't come home for the past two nights, and I haven't spoken to him since we had gotten into a heated argument some days ago. Caine was known for pulling disappearing acts, and although it was nothing new to me, I didn't condone it and knew that I deserved better.

I have a huge meeting today and I am due downtown in a little over an hour. After shedding a few tears and trying to get my mind right, I stood up, straightened my face and decided to get to it.

At 26 years of age, I have always been independent and driven. I fell in love with music at a very young age, and dedicated myself to the craft since way back when. Today, I have a meeting with Royalty

Records, a big name record label. Almost a year ago, I was approached in Los Angeles, after one of my performances by an A&R rep. I have been back and forth over a contract agreement for the past few months. I was due in today to sign my contract and meet with my development team, so we could get the ball rolling to push out my first single, and the timeline for my first album. Today was a busy day and I had fully expected Caine to be there on time, so that I could handle my business. I loved traveling, meeting new people, and being able to perform in front of them repeatedly. However every time I came back home, I had to deal with Caine's attitude. I hated that I couldn't just come home to relax and unwind with my man. All I wanted was for the one that I loved and supported to do the same for me.

I walked across the bathroom and picked up my phone from the floor; as hard as it had been thrown, there was no damage, thanks to the hard case that surrounded it. Taking a deep breath, I tried to get my thoughts together and my heartbeat steady. I hated to be dependent on anybody, but with my car being out of commission, I had no choice but to rely on Caine to get me where I needed to go until my insurance paid out. I had called and texted him nonstop since yesterday afternoon to remind him of the time to be there. His inconsiderate ass never even responded with a simple text to let me know what the deal was. The least that he could have done was texted back and say that he couldn't make it. I logged onto my Uber account and requested a ride; my pride wouldn't allow me to call anybody else. Either one of my best friends, Cass or Dezi, would hop up and take me with no problem. My younger sister or older brother would even drop whatever they were doing to get me to this meeting, but I still couldn't bring myself to let them know that once again, Caine had been unreliable.

I gathered my things and made sure that I looked presentable. I was sporting a cute, olive green, calf-length dress that hugged my petite frame, along with some peep toe pumps, I slid on my jewelry, touched up my makeup, fingered my wand curls, and I was ready to go. I decided to push all of the bullshit to the back of my mind and focus on what lay ahead. I had dedicated my entire life to my craft and it was finally paying off big time, so I refused to let anything ruin my happy day. Caine and all of his bullshit could kick rocks for the time being, but please believe once all of my business was handled, he would be feeling my wrath. I was tired of his bullshit and I'm at the point in my life where he could either get with the program or keep it pushing. I looked down at my phone and was notified that my Uber was outside, so I grabbed my things and rushed out of the door.

With fifteen minutes to spare, I made it to my meeting; I grabbed my phone and shot a text to my manager. Jamie had been my manager for the past two and a half years, but we had known one another since middle school. She had made all of this possible; I truly owed her everything. She busted her ass and bent over backwards repeatedly to get my name out there. I had worked with all of the Bay Area greats, and now I'm looking to get to work with some bigger names. People always said that I had a phenomenal voice; they described it as soulful and yet chilling, to the point where I could cause goose bumps with every note. I knew that my voice was good, but honestly, I did it just because I loved the feeling I got whenever I sang. Jamie approached me with a huge smile on her face.

"Hey Chocolate Candie!" Jamie called out. She had been calling me that since we met and the nickname stuck. We proceeded to the suite where the meeting was to be held and checked in with the secretary, who notified her boss of our arrival. I took a seat and waited to be called upon.

Jamie looked at me with a huge smile on her face. I laughed because she was probably happier than I was; I was excited, but I was more nervous. For years, I had been in the studio, doing shows, photo shoots, video shoots, and appearances. I had been doing things on my own time, my own dime, and within my own comfort zone. However, I knew that now under a label, I would have to take direction from somebody else, so I was definitely nervous at this new chapter in my life.

"Candie, Mr. Simpson and the rest are ready for you now," the tall brunette secretary announced. I stood up and looked back at Jamie as she gathered her bag, and we walked into the conference room.

Chapter 2: Caine

I rode through the city, my music blasting, with no real destination; I looked at my phone as it rang for about the fiftieth time. Candie had been blowing me up all morning, but I wasn't trying to hear shit that she had to say. If she wanted to get to where she was going, she could figure it out. I told her ass to go and get a rental the other day when she got back from her three-day tour in Washington. Candie wanted to live her life freely, and do whatever she wanted to do on some independent woman shit. If she wanted to carry on as if she didn't have a man carrying her ass all over the damn place, then she could keep on doing her, while I did me. I pulled up to the block and spotted my nigga, Josh; he had been my best friend since the sandbox. We had played Pop Warner football together, basketball leagues in middle school at Tassa Recreation Center, and jumped in the game together in high school. He was more than a friend; he was family.

I parked at the curb, hopped out, looked around and it was quiet still, but I knew that in about an hour or so, the block would be moving. I looked at my watch; I had a studio session at two, but it was only eleven, so I had time to fuck around. "Sup with my nigga, Candie Caine?" Josh asked, with a chuckle.

He knew I hated when niggas called me that. Niggas thought the shit was cute, because Candie was my girl, so they wanted to play. I hated that name. "Fuck you, nigga, that's what ya' mama was moaning in my ear this morning," I said as I threw a fake jab that Josh blocked. We dapped each other up as I grabbed the blunt from behind my ear and fired it up.

"Nah, what's up with my nigga Cocaine Cowboy? Ain't Candie supposed to sign that contract today? I know you happy," he said, with a slight grin.

"Happy for what? Nigga that shit don't have nothing to do with me. It ain't my money; shit … all that shit gonna bring is more niggas in her face, and her ass about to be away from home even more than she already is," I said.

Josh looked at me for a second and shook his head. "Let me ask you this, African, do you love your bitch? Like, why are you even with her if you always tripping off what she doing, especially when you out here doing your own thing?" he asked.

I hit the blunt and thought about what he asked me. Shit, of course, I loved Candie. I loved her to death, but she was moving along with her life and I'm not going to lie; I felt as if she didn't need me anymore.

When Candie and I first started dating, she was doing her thing music wise. We met in the studio and from the day I met her, we just had that vibe. I loved her voice and she always had a way of making me feel as if I could conquer the world. She was my world and I wanted to make her my wife one day, but right now, we were in two separate places in life. I sat in the studio with her day in and day out, making beats, working on our dreams. From open mics to local showcases, we had done it all together as a team, but now Candie was all over the place and she had left me here in the hood. I made good money doing my music and I had been grinding for years. I had real niggas that fucked with me, but I wanted to be bigger than Oakland, bigger than the Bay Area. I was tired of being around the crab in a barrel ass niggas; I wanted to expand and I couldn't be complacent. I was a hood nigga, but my granny had taught me to dream big. No matter what I had done in my life, I knew that this wasn't it for me. What I needed was for Candie to believe in me, as I had believed in her, but how did I explain all of that to her without sounding like a hater? I chopped it up on the block for a minute and then dipped, so that I could get to the studio on time. It was about to be a long day in the lab, but I had to get to the money.

After my studio session, I was tired as shit; I hadn't been home in a couple of days and I knew that Candie was going to go ape shit on my ass. I didn't want to go home and fight; I wanted to just relax, get a warm meal, and climb up into some wet-wet, before I passed out for the rest of the night. I pulled up into the driveway and bounced out of my whip, prepping myself for what lay on the other side of the door. Soon as I opened the door, the aroma of food and weed hit my nose and my stomach growled, reminding me that I hadn't eaten all day. I could hear music blasting from the kitchen and voices as well. I was slipping, because I didn't even notice the other cars parked outside; I dropped my computer bag by the door and continued toward where I heard the commotion. I walked into the kitchen and it looked like a full-blown dinner party was occurring. Candie was standing next to the stove frying chicken. Her younger sister, Honey, best friends Cass and Dezi, Josh's girl, Lacey, and her brother's girl, Taylor, were all sitting or standing around in full party mode. There were bottles of Hennessy and Grey Goose on the table and it was smoky as hell in there.

I gave a general head nod to everybody in the room and walked up to Candie, smacking her ass. She was looking good as hell in her leggings, with her hair sitting on top of her head in a messy bun and her sports bra. Staring at her plump booty had me on brick status. I leaned over and kissed her on her neck, pressing my hard on into her butt cheeks. She stiffened slightly to my touch, so I knew that she was pissed at me but she wasn't the type of chick that aired our dirty laundry to the public. She would act like wasn't shit wrong and then go smooth in on a nigga once we were alone.

"Damn it's a full-blown pussy party in this motherfucker, I guess daddy wasn't invited," I said, whispering in her ear, as she turned towards me with her breast brushing against my chest. I could see the fire dancing in her eyes as she looked into my face.

"Why do you need to be invited to a party at your own home? If you had been here, you would have known that we were celebrating my new contract. There are *some* people that are actually proud of me," she said rolling her eyes.

"Cut that shit out, Candie." I leaned down and kissed her lips. I knew she wasn't feeling a nigga right now, but I planned to break her down. I had missed her little ass and I needed her to warm up to a nigga, instead of being all cold and sassy.

"Whatever, Caine, the guys are in the garage shooting pool."

I nodded my head and dipped off toward the garage. I stepped into the garage and it was even smokier than the kitchen was, these niggas were out here blowing it down. I looked around and saw Josh, Candie's brother, Sincere, and Laz, Dezi's boyfriend posted around the garage, smoking and shooting pool. There was money on the table, so I knew these niggas were betting big money. I grabbed a beer off the table and popped it open.

"What's good with my niggas?" I asked, as I copped a seat on the couch and got ready to watch the entertainment; shit was about to get funny. These niggas loved to gamble, but it always ended up coming damn near to blows, because somebody's drunk ass always accused somebody of cheating one way or another. "I like how ain't none of you niggas call me and tell me there was a party at my house," I said, while taking a swig from my Corona.

Josh looked at me and shook his head.

"Nigga, how you ain't know there was going to be a party and you live here? Shit, you should have been throwing the bitch considering the occasion," Sincere said, eyeing me.

I knew Candie probably hadn't mentioned that I hadn't been home in a few days, but these niggas weren't stupid, and I knew I had to clean shit up some. These were my niggas and if I couldn't keep it real with my niggas, then who could I keep it real with?

I shook my head. "Man, I been hella busy and just left the studio. Between my shit and Candie's shit, we kind of missed each other today. Plus, we ain't been one hunnid since she came back from Washington the other day," I said, as Laz passed me an unlit blunt. I pulled a lighter from my pocket and fired it up. I tapped the blunt and nodded my head; this nigga stayed with some good ass weed. I looked up and all these niggas were staring me in my face as if I had sprouted two heads or something. "Man, you niggas bugging, ain't y'all running a game? Damn!" I said, feeling uncomfortable under their gazes.

"Don't lose your bitch behind your pride, my nigga, you ain't going to like it when she finds somebody that appreciates her and supports her more than you," Laz said as he approached the table to take his shot.

I let his words sink in. I never spoke on how I really felt to anybody, because I don't want to sound like a bitch. I'm a real nigga and I just like to handle shit my own way.

"I hear you, my nigga, but don't trip; Candie ain't going nowhere."

For the rest of the night we chilled and got lifted. We ended up going back into the house with the ladies and continuing the party. Candie was very distant all night and I started to feel bad. I knew she felt as if I didn't care, but I was proud of Candie, because she deserved everything that she had accomplished. I might not always show it, but I really admired her determination. She busted her ass day in and day out and still put up with all of my bullshit. I'd be in my feelings sometimes; loving a woman could have any man acting crazy, but loving a beautiful, successful woman would have a man on some wild shit.

I sat in my home studio, checking emails before going to bed. Honestly, I was procrastinating because I knew once I walked into that room; Candie was going to go in on a nigga. I had been acting like an asshole, but I planned to make it up to her this weekend. After checking and responding to emails, I shut my computer down and stretched, I would let Candie talk her shit for a minute but afterwards, she was going to lose that attitude though. I was trying to get up in something tight and wet and it wasn't going to work if she wasn't going to be cooperative. I hadn't fucked my bitch in almost two weeks. I can't lie and act as if I've been a hundred percent faithful. I mean, random pussy is cool when you're just looking for a nut, but ain't nothing like your pussy, the one you know is reserved just for you. Candie's pussy was designed for me, even if she married another nigga, his dick wouldn't fit her like mine; that shit there got Cocaine written all in it.

I walked into the room and found Candie laying across the bed with her Beats headphones on and humming aloud. I knew that she was writing and I swear, seeing my baby in her mode was sexy as hell to me. I stood in the doorway and just listened to her voice; I felt chills overcome me as I let her voice soothe my soul. It was crazy how her voice still had that effect on me.

Candie turned around and looked at me as I smiled at her sexy ass. I could tell she was tipsy, because her eyes were low and she had a slight scowl on her face. She wasn't giving me any slack tonight. I wasn't tripping though, because I knew that I hadn't been on my best behavior. I didn't want to have to fuck Pamela tonight, but I might just be on my own.

"Why you staring at me like that? You miss daddy?" I asked, winking at her as she rolled her eyes and sat up on the bed, tucking her legs up under her.

"Nigga, don't come up in here acting like shit's all good. Hell no, I don't miss your black ass. The fuck made you bring your dirty ass home for tonight? That bitch got tired of you?"

I shook my head; Candie's mouth could get reckless at times.

I walked over to the bed and sat on the edge. "Cut it out, baby, I wasn't with no bitch, man. Sometimes I just need a break, shit. I don't be trying to come home and argue all the damn time; that shit be draining the fuck out of me," I said, rubbing on her leg, Candie pushed my hand back and snaked her neck. I

18

didn't understand how black girls did that crazy shit without breaking that motherfucker; it must have been some kind of technique to that shit.

"Nigga you sitting here talking about what's draining? I travel fifty million times a month and every time I bring my ass back to this bitch, you got a fucking problem. You think I want to come home and hear a grown ass man bitch all damn night? You sit in here sounding like a jealous broad, the way your ass be complaining and shit."

I stared at her with fire in my eyes and she stared back at me with the same inferno dancing in hers. I pushed her back onto the bed and got right into her face; my hand wrapped quickly around her throat, applying slight pressure. "Bitch, watch your mouth when you speaking to me, my nigga. I'm not one of them hoe ass niggas you travel on tour with. So I suggest you choose your words wisely when you speak to me," I said, with my teeth clenched in anger.

Candie's gaze never wavered though; if looks could kill, I would be one dead ass nigga. I released my hold on her and stood up, heading to the bathroom, but as soon as I got to the bathroom door, I felt something heavy hit the back of my head. I instinctively grabbed the back of my head and felt moisture. I looked down in shock; this bitch had thrown her damn laptop at me. I turned around and she was standing on top of the bed, looking as if she was ready to rumble. I wasn't even about to play into her games tonight, she was drunk and mad. I walked into the bathroom, grabbed a hand towel and wet it, and then applied it to the lump in the back of my head. I walked out of the bathroom, took one last look at Candie, and walked out of the house. I didn't trust sleeping with her crazy ass tonight.

Candie could get very vindictive when she wanted to; when we fought, she would get childish as hell. The last time we got into a big argument, she had acted as if she was over it and all was cool. The night after we had stayed in for a romantic night alone, and I don't care what nobody say, her ass slipped me something. She had cooked a nigga a meal fit for a king; we had popped a big bottle of Rémy, and we were having fun. Every so often, I would catch her eyeing me real funny like; the last thing I remember is her going down to give me head. When I woke up the next afternoon, I looked in the mirror to find her crazy ass had cut patches in my damn head and shaved off all my facial hair, eyebrows included. Bitch had me walking around looking like a naked mole rat for weeks. Shit, I'm rather sure she never even gave me head that night. To this day, my niggas clown me about that shit. So tonight, I was going to give her space, because I didn't want to hurt her little ass, and I didn't know what she had going on in her retarded ass head. I was trying to be a good man and stay home, but shit, her ass was on bullshit and I don't have time.

Chapter 3: Candie

Walking through the car dealership, I was feeling some type of way. I really couldn't shake how I was feeling, but I had gotten my ass up to handle my business. I was determined to find a car today, because tomorrow, I was due to fly to L.A. for the week and I didn't want to come back and still be car less. Things with Caine and I had been shaky lately, but he had surprisingly accompanied me today to go car shopping. I really did appreciate it, but the vibe was just all off. Caine stood off to the side, admiring a big body Benz; I wasn't really attracted to the foreign shit. I had my eye on a Jeep Wrangler and I wanted to add all of the extras, my big dilemma is color. "Baby, can you come here please?" I asked, calling out to Caine, I opened the door to an all-black Wrangler and I swear I felt my heart flutter. This truck was everything to me, and I wanted it like now.

Caine came over to me and started looking over the truck. He nodded his head in approval, as if I was actually waiting for him to give it to me. "So are you sure this is what you want? Have you checked the safety report on it? How many miles do you get per gallon? Looks aren't everything, so I mean, what's up?" he asked, looking over the interior and the auto manual.

I rolled my eyes. *This nigga always wanted to fuck up my vibe.* I placed my hand on my hip and looked at Caine. "I checked all of that online, babe, and this is the truck I want so are you going to grab the man and have him draw up the paperwork? Or are you going to sit here and give me a lecture on some shit that I've already checked up on?"

Caine looked at me and shook his head. I smiled at him and went back to sit behind the wheel, as he went to grab the salesman.

Pulling off in my brand new Jeep, I was on cloud nine. I was happy that I didn't have to depend on Caine's unreliable ass and didn't have to rack up any more time with Uber. This Jeep was everything; I couldn't wait to send it off to get my add-ons while I was gone. I was pushing 90 on I-880, headed to my brother's house. We had a lunch date and I was excited to spend some time with him, because I had been moving so much that I hadn't had any bonding time with him. Growing up, my siblings and I were super close; our single father raised us.

Our mother had run off when we were small and had never come back; once she left, our father wrote her off from our lives. He never went to look for her, never went to her family and asked them to take us in, or anything of the sorts. He used to say that if she wanted to be there, then that's where she would be; he never down talked her, but after a while, she was never even brought up. As a man, he stood up and raised three children and we had all come out pretty great, if you asked me. Growing up in Oakland, some people don't make it to eighteen; some ended up in jail doing numbers at a young age, and then some ended up strung out on drugs. We may not have made the best decisions in everything that we did, but we definitely were better off than we could have been.

I drove to Sincere's house with a bunch of things on my mind, I needed to be focused on my trip, but thoughts of my relationship with Caine were eating at me. I woke up day after day, feeling that maybe our relationship had run its course, but there was part of me that couldn't give up the fight for my man. I had put in so much over the past four years; I wasn't looking for another nigga, I was more so looking for new things in the nigga I already had. Thing is, I wasn't sure if Caine was capable of being on the same page as I was, that's why I needed to talk to my brother. Sincere was a close friend to Caine, but first, he was my big brother; he would tell me the real and wouldn't sugarcoat it. I pulled up to his three-bedroom home and sat there for a minute, just staring at the home. Sin had been through so much; I was glad that he was still here with us, and he was finally living the life he deserved.

A couple of years ago, Sin was out here on one; he was fucking around with some crazy bitch and she had that nigga tripping. One day the bitch came home and told him that she was pregnant. My brother was excited; he had been working for about a year, and he had been put on permanently. His job wasn't a corporate gig, but he worked great hours and made good money. For months, my brother doted on that trifling bitch, making sure that she or the baby wouldn't need anything. He picked up extra hours to save up for a house and had bought a second car, so that they wouldn't be reliant on each other to get around.

One night, Sin had left work not feeling well; when he got home, he found his girlfriend laid up with another nigga on the couch. That night, Sin snapped; he damn near beat the nigga to death and was taken to jail. My brother did five months in the county jail behind that shit; while he was in there, he found out that the baby he was expecting didn't even belong to him.

Once he was released, Sincere went through a rough patch; he had fallen into a horrible funk, and it seemed as if nothing could pull him out of it. Sin had saved enough money before the incident to buy a house, and I helped him find one to purchase. I thought that buying his own house would pull him out of the funk, but it didn't. My brother was out here getting high off syrup and pills, hustling on the streets and shit. Sin was never just a square ass nigga, but he wasn't the type to hang out on the corners, slinging drugs and getting high either. One day I had gone to Sin's house and found him laid out on the floor; my brother was unresponsive. I called 911 and told them my brother had taken an abundance of pills. They pumped his stomach right there on the floor of his bedroom and saved his life. Sincere was sent to the hospital; he stayed for two days, before they hauled him off to John George Psychiatric Hospital, where he stayed for three months. My dad, Honey, and I went up there faithfully to visit with him; we did family therapy sessions and anything that would help to bring my brother back. Caine and Josh were also there for him throughout the entire ordeal.

After repeated tests and therapy sessions, my brother had improved greatly and seemed like he was back to his normal self. The doctors' finally cleared him to go home, but prescribed him with meds for depression and assigned him to outpatient therapy. Now Sincere was back working legally, and you would never know that he had almost ended his life two years ago.

I honked the horn and waited for him to come outside, while I checked my email. I confirmed with Jamie that I had received my itinerary, and would be ready and on time, first thing tomorrow morning. I looked up as Sin walked to the passenger side of my Jeep; my brother was a very handsome man. He was only two years older than I was, but sometimes, he had the vibe of an old man. Sincere was the color of toasted almonds and his brown skin glowed with a golden touch. He was tall, rather stocky, and his dreads were neat and fell freely down his back. Sin had light brown eyes, one deep dimple in his left cheek, and he kept a short goatee that always stayed lined perfectly. "What's up, sis?" Sin said, as he climbed into the passenger seat. He looked around the inside of my whip smiling.

"Shit... What's up with you, nigga?" I replied, backing out of the driveway, heading back towards the freeway.

"I see you finally went to cop. You must have been tired of depending on Caine," he said, firing up a fresh blunt.

"Damn nigga... I ain't had the car three hours and you already polluting it with that shit," I said, scrunching up my nose at the pungent smell of marijuana. I didn't know the difference between cookies, Kush or purple; I didn't know what made the weed that they sold at the cannabis club any better than the weed sold on the block. I just knew that I wasn't fucking up my voice over some weed; I drank, but I didn't fuck with anything else.

I pulled into the parking garage and it took a couple of minutes to find a parking space. I hated parking in the garages sometimes, because they always had those dumb ass compact stalls everywhere on the first two levels, and my truck wasn't exactly what you called compact. Sin and I stepped out and walked side by side to the street; we were headed inside The Cheesecake Factory in San Francisco. I couldn't wait to get seated and get that good ass bread; I was starving from running around all day.

Once we were seated, I checked my phone to see if I had any missed calls or texts from Caine. I had texted him when I first made it to Sin's house to see if he wanted to spend some time together tonight, considering that I would be gone away on business for an entire week. I hated when I reached out to him and he made no effort to respond. That shit irked my nerves. Sin had stepped away to use the restroom, so I used the time to call Caine, since he wasn't responding to texts. I called Caine twice and he didn't answer either call. I placed my phone back in my bag and dove into the plate of bread the hostess had set on the table.

"Your server will be right with you," the hostess said, before turning and walking away.

Sincere came back to the table and sat down, grabbing the piece of bread out of my hand. "Damn Sin, it's a whole damn plate, why you had to take mine?" I whined because my taste buds were anticipating the buttery bread.

"Yours was buttered and those aren't, you can butter up another piece, this the only piece I want," he said seriously. I squinted my eyes at him because he was so damn spoiled. I was his younger sister, but he knew I would do anything for him, just as I knew he would do anything for me.

"Whatever, Sin, so what's been up with you, playa?" I asked, picking up another piece and buttering both sides, before placing the warm delight into my mouth.

"I'm good sis, life is good, but I think I'm ready to have a little me running around this motherfucka'. Thing is, Taylor is almost done with school and ready to start her career, but I'm ready to start a family, you feel me?" he said, sipping from his glass of water.

I nodded my head and thought for a moment, before speaking. I knew his past relationship haunted him at times and he was hurt behind the treachery of his ex bitch. However, I didn't want him to rush anything and mess up the life he was making with his girlfriend, Taylor. She was a good girl; she was ambitious, pretty, and loyal. I knew that she was the girl for my brother, but I also knew that she wasn't ready to give up her freedom yet for a baby.

I paused for a moment as the waitress came to our table and took our drink and appetizer orders. Once she was gone, I took a sip from my water then prepared myself to keep it one hundred with my brother. "Look Sin, I know that you low key have baby fever right now, but I think you and Taylor should wait. She's fresh out of school and is ready to at least get her foot in the door with her career, before she takes the time out to have a baby," I said, looking into his face to gauge his reaction to what I was saying. "I say to at least wait another year. You can talk to her about planning a family, but you should make sure that you guys are really solid, before you take that step and add an innocent child into the mix. I know you love and trust her and I love her as well, just take a little time, bruh," I said as our drinks came and the waitress took our food orders.

Sin's face was scrunched up as he ordered his food, so I know he wasn't feeling what I had said, but shit, I hoped he would take heed.

Once our food had been ordered, we jumped right back into our conversation. "I ain't trying to wait. Shit, I'm almost thirty, and I don't have a little shorty yet. I never saw myself being a family guy, until the day Vanessa told me she was pregnant. For seven months I was the happiest nigga walking. I didn't care if it was a boy or a girl; I was just juiced to be sharing a child with the bitch that I loved," Sin said, grabbing a tempura shrimp and stuffing it in his mouth.

"I know, Sin. I remember. I never even thought you wanted to settle down like that. I mean, you was ever no dog ass nigga, but you liked doing you. If you are ready to do all that now after all you went through with that bitch, Vanessa, then I'm rocking with you. Just make sure that you and Taylor are on the same page," I said, looking at his buzzing phone on the table. I saw Caine's name flash across the screen, I grabbed my phone from my purse and saw that he had never called me back or even responded to my text.

When Sincere answered his phone, I made a hand gesture at my neck and shook my head to let him know not to tell him that he was with me. I watched Sin's face trying to hear what Caine was saying; I tapped my foot out of anger, because Caine could be so inconsiderate.

Once Sin hung up the phone, I gave him that "nigga spill the beans" look. He shook his head and chuckled. "Nigga, you know that I ain't about to get in the middle of y'all shit. So you better sip your drink and hit him yourself," he said.

I shook my head and grabbed my phone, calling Caine again. "Bitch ass nigga," I said, as he ignored yet another call, so I sent him a text.

Me: *Why do your retarded ass keep ignoring my calls, you must be with a bitch since you can't hit me back. Maybe I will go to L.A. and never come back. DUMB ASS NIGGA*

I placed my phone back into my bag and turned back to my brother. His ass was staring at me with a weird look on his face. "What?" I asked irritated to the max.

"Don't be mad at me foo', I didn't do it. What y'all going to do? I see shit ain't been right between y'all in months and that's my nigga, but you my little sister first. I think maybe y'all should take a break and see where that leaves you," Sin said, as our food finally landed at our table.

I shook my head. "I'm not trying to take no breaks, Sin. If we break up, that's it. Ain't no back and forth shit, we too old to for that. If that nigga wanted to be with me, he would get his mind right. I just want to go back to how life used to be, Sin, back when Caine and I were inseparable and I could feel he loved me," I said, with tears threatening to spill from my eyes.

Sincere reached over and grabbed my hand, as I used my napkin to catch the hardheaded tears that fell even after I told them not to. "Look sis, if you are going to fight for your relationship then do that, but don't be stupid. Niggas are going to fuck up, but you have to choose when enough is enough for you. Caine ain't the only nigga out here and he definitely ain't the only nigga that will ever love you."

I nodded my head at Sin and then dug into my food. I let my brother's words marinate as I devoured my Louisiana Chicken Pasta. The food was so good that we stayed relatively quiet for the remainder of the meal making small talk. After I finished my food, I placed a dessert order and then excused myself to the restroom. On my way there, I caught the eye of some bright ass bitch eyeing me. Anybody who knew me knew that I hated to be stared at. My sister always thought that was funny, because most people recognized me from shows and flyers and stared, trying to think of where they knew me. This bitch though, was definitely staring for another reason. I snaked my neck and placed my hand out like, "bitch what"? The yellow bitch smirked and turned back to her table, while I kept pushing to my destination.

I stepped out of the stall and walked to the sink to wash my hands and touch up my makeup. As I pulled my lipstick from my bag, the door to the restroom opened up and lo and behold, in walked "light bright". I rolled my eyes and turned back towards the mirror.

"Bitch, I bet you ain't about to keep rolling them bitches, I know that much," she said, placing her hand on her hip.

"Excuse me, do I know you? Like, who the fuck are you?" I asked.

"Nah, you don't know me like that, Candie, but the name is Joy. I'm sure you might have heard about me though."

I rolled my eyes at this pathetic bitch. "Girl please, your mama ain't taught you any manners, huh? She didn't teach you that it was rude to stare? Not to speak to strangers and most importantly, never to write a check that your ass can't cash?" I asking, placing my things back in my bag and returning it back to the crook of my arm.

She stared for a moment; apparently trying to find whatever words she was about to throw at me. I sighed and walked right past her, before I turned around one last time, facing her. "Another thing ... if you were approaching me to tell me that you're fucking my nigga, then keep it to yourself, boo. Nobody likes a tattle tale," I said, and walked right out of the door.

Bitches killed me; always trying to approach a nigga's broad to rub in their face that they are fucking her nigga. The shit was so classless, like damn; if you know about his bitch then what is the point of telling her that you fucking him? Like, bitch, you wrong for doing it for one, and you wrong for spreading that nigga business for two. I hated how hoes thought that doing this would make them break up, and then it would be her turn. Musical chairs ass bitches; clearly, they didn't take notes when Webbie dropped "Gutta Bitch". I shook my head, irritated even more as I walked up to the table.

Sin looked up at me and stood as he placed a tip down and handed me my dessert. "What's your issue, your nigga called back?" he asked.

"Hell no," I said, as I filled him in on the fiasco that occurred in the bathroom.

Sin just shook his head. We drove back to his house in silence as we listened to Rick Ross' "Black Dollar".

I pulled into Sin's driveway and put the gear in park, leaving the engine running. All I wanted to do was climb into bed and get ready for my flight in the morning.

Sin unfastened his seatbelt and the turned towards me. "Caine wanted me to go out with him tonight, but I ain't going. If you want to hang around here, you're more than welcome," he said.

I gave him a slight smile. "I'm good big bruh, I'm just going to go home and rest up. I have a million things to do once I get to L.A., so I will catch you when I get back," I said, leaning over to kiss his cheek.

Sin nodded and opened his door. "Don't let that nigga stress you, Candie."

I nodded my head and once he had made it onto his porch, I pulled off and headed home.

I walked in the house feeling as if the world was weighing on my shoulders. I placed my purse on the chair next to the window, and headed into the kitchen to grab a snack, before I retired to the bedroom. I grabbed some Heath Bar ice cream from the freezer and scooped some into a bowl; I grabbed a cold can of cream soda and my Black-Out cake from the restaurant and walked to my bedroom. I definitely ate like a fat girl, but I barely gained any weight. I took advantage of the free eating as much as I could; I hoped that it wouldn't catch up to me anytime soon. I stripped out of my clothes, climbed into my bed in just my bra and panties, and turned on my DVR to catch up on my new favorite show, *Quantico*. I was usually too busy to watch television, but at nights when I was able to chill at home, I usually gravitated to the previously aired shows. I would spend hours watching the season. I cuddled up under my covers and dove into my dessert.

I shifted in my sleep as I heard my bedroom door open up. I turned over, looked at the time, and saw that it was after three in the morning. I instantly got pissed. I had to be up in an hour so that I could make it to the airport on time, and this nigga wanted to walk up in this bitch as if it was three in the afternoon, being hella loud and turning on lights and shit. I sat up in the bed and glared at Caine; he was clearly drunk, but that wasn't an excuse. I had given him the option to spend time with me and he chose not to, so what he wasn't about to do was walk up in here like it was good, after he shook me and then interrupted my fucking sleep.

"Really Caine? Like ... this is what the fuck we doing now?" I yelled.

"Man ... Candie, gon' with that bullshit, I'm not trying to hear your mouth tonight. Don't you got a fucking plane to catch or something? I just knew your ass would be gone by now, shit!" he said, turning away from me and undressing.

I cocked my head to the side. "Motherfucker, first of all, it ain't nighttime anymore. You been missed that train baby, and don't worry, I will be gone soon enough. I hate you. I swear I need to find a new nigga that know how to act. I don't know why I still fuck with your bum ass."

I pushed the covers off me and stood up. I was already packed, so I walked over to my armoire and grabbed some intimates to throw on after I got out of the shower.

I was so damn tired of Caine and his shit. I swear I didn't want to come home after L.A.; I would swoop up Cass and Dezi, and get the hell on somewhere. I was snatching shit up and talking shit, I hated how Caine acted towards me. "You know what, nigga; I'm tired of this shit!" I yelled, throwing a bottle of body wash at his ass. Caine did something to me and I couldn't control my anger when he pissed me off.

Caine turned towards me eyes low and blood shot red, but I was waiting for his ass to jump. "Tired of what, Candie? Huh, tell me what the fuck you're tired of?" he said calmly.

He was so calm that my words got choked up inside me. I stared at him wondering how things between us got to this point; at one time, I was so in love with him. He was sexy and talented, and we were such a perfect fit. Caine stood there, looking good enough to eat. His caramel skin was bright and flawless, his brown eyes were bloodshot, but and wide, and his lips were soft and plump, surrounded by a gorgeous five o'clock shadow. I stared at his broad chest and admired his many tattoos. Caine's biceps were large and strong looking, and I wished that instead of arguing, he was using that energy to pick me up and fuck me until I tapped out. Instead, we were here squaring off as if we hated each other.

I opened my mouth to answer his question. "Tired of how you been acting towards me. If I'm not the bitch that you want to fuck with, then be my guest to go find that hoe, because I'm not into keeping a nigga that don't want to be kept," I said. I was so mad that I was shaking. I was talking all of this shit because it was really how I felt, but at the same time, I didn't know what I would do if this nigga decided to just walk the fuck out and leave me. I stood there frozen in time, waiting on Caine to say something, but he never uttered a word. He simply walked out the room without so much as a second look.

Tears threatened to fall from my eyes, but I held my ground and didn't let them. I grabbed my things and continued toward the bathroom to take my shower. In the shower, I let the tears flow freely. This relationship had run its course and I didn't want to stay around, waiting to kill each other, because we grew to hate one another. I was making my mind up, when I was finished with my business in Los Angeles; I would come home and pack my shit up. The majority of my business was based in L.A.; the label was out there, studios and all. It would be a fresh start for me and I would be able to focus on my music. The change of scenery and throwing myself into my work would help me to keep my mind off Caine.

I stepped out of the shower with relief, because I now had a plan. I couldn't keep walking on eggshells in my own home. Wondering what day Caine would come home, finally say that he was done with me, and then walk out. Before I put myself through that, I would leave my damn self. I knew that he dealt with other bitches behind my back and that shit was eating me up every day. I had been Caine's ride or die for the past four years, but I refused to confuse that with being a dummy. I didn't know what he had going with these other hoes and I wasn't about to wait around, let him choose another bitch over me, come home one day and throw me the deuces.

I dried myself off and applied lotion to my body, before slipping on my panties and bra. I took a deep breath and sat down on the bed, before pulling on a pair of knee high socks and then my Adidas joggers, with a tank top and the matching hoodie. I placed my half-carat diamond studs in my ears, and then made sure that I had everything I needed before I took off. I grabbed my phone, charger, and keys then headed out the door. When I passed through the living room, Caine was sprawled across the couch, smoking a blunt. I walked past him and didn't even glance in his direction as I grabbed my handbag off the chair.

"Bitch," I said, as I slammed the door, hopped in my Jeep and peeled out of the driveway, headed to Jamie's. I would have just parked in the daily lot at the airport, but Jamie insisted on taking an Uber there and I just park at her house. I let Nipsey Hussle's voice put me in the zone as I drove, hoping to get my mind right,

I would be working with a team of new producers. Once I touched down in the City of Angels, I wanted to start looking for a place to live as well. Maybe a nice condo or something, but whatever the case, I was ready to grab the bull by the horns and take on whatever life decided to throw at me.

Chapter 4: Caine

I woke up on the couch with a banging ass headache. "Bruh," I groaned, as I struggled to sit up. My muscles were hella tight and my stomach was fucked up. I stood up to my feet and went straight to the bathroom. That Henny was doing voodoo on my damn guts; I grabbed the air freshener from under the sink, my phone out of my pocket, and prepared myself to take a much-needed gangster. I pulled up my Instagram and the first thing I saw was *this* bitch. Candie posed with her titties damn near popping out of her shirt, and some weak ass caption, talking about some damn, *New Residence. New Me. These niggas ain't ready for the heat I'm about to bring.* This bitch loved to act up on these social sites. Soon as we got into a fight, she would post hella subliminals and have me ready to beat her ass. I clicked on her page and she had been posting shit all morning as if she was on some single shit. I didn't know what the fuck her problem was, but she had me fucked up. I instantly shot her ass a text.

Me: *Bitch, quit playing with me before I smash to LA and put my foot in your ass, you wanna be single? Is that what you want?*

Candie: *Caine continue to do you and don't worry 'bout me boo. You wasn't worried last night, you weren't worried this morning, and you for damn sure ain't been worried while you out there fucking all these random ass hoes. How about you worry about wrapping your dick up, bitch!*

This broad was really pushing my buttons. I see I was about to have to show her, instead of doing all of this irrelevant ass talking. I was already pissed off behind taking a fucking loss yesterday, and this bitch wanted to keep fucking with me. It was all good though; I was about to see how much talking Candie was about to be doing soon enough. I finished handling my duties in the bathroom and got up out of there, before I died from the stench. That shit that had just come up out of me was lethal. I sprayed my way up out that bitch and walked into the room so that I could take a shower and catch the next thing smoking to L.A.

One thing I couldn't stand about Candie, was that she was always assuming some dumb shit. Candie was dramatic as fuck; she liked to yell, curse, and act a damn fool when she was upset. Then as soon as I say some rude shit or just ignore her ass, she swears that our relationship is over. I tell her all the time that couples fight and that's normal for relationships, but I swear she lived in a fantasy world, filled with spice, sugar, and everything nice or however that dumb ass saying goes.

Once I stepped out of the shower, I logged onto Southwest to find the next flight out to LAX. I shot a text to Josh and let him know my move; he offered to come with me, but I told him that I was straight. I didn't have anything scheduled for the next two days, so I was able to leave and not have to worry about rushing back. Once I had booked my flight, I had about an hour to pack a small bag and get to the airport before my flight boarded. Next, I sent Candie's assistant, Jamie, a text and asked for the address to the studio. I told her that I was sending Candie some flowers and to keep it a secret.

Once she sent me the address, I grabbed my bag ad was out the door. I hopped in my whip and checked my phone as it chimed with a Snapchat notification. I tapped the icon and instantly, I was staring into one of the prettiest pussies I had seen in a minute. My dick jumped at the sight, but I was trying to keep my mind on the task at hand. I started the car and adjusted my dick in my pants as I pulled out and headed towards Oakland Airport.

It was tough trying to be a stand up nigga when I hadn't felt my own bitch's pussy in over a month. On the other hand, I had all these bitches throwing the pussy at me, placing it on silver platters, dressing it up with greenery, and handing it to a nigga like it was mine to keep. Shit, a nigga is going to be a nigga. I can only say no to so many hoes, before my dick catches up to me and reminds me that it needs hydration to survive. I mean, damn, I'm a young handsome nigga and I had needs; I still liked to get my dick wet, despite whatever Candie thought. Temptation was a bitch; I don't care how much you love your bitch, you going to dip in another bitch from time to time. Thoughts of pussy ran through my mind as I boarded my flight and found a seat by the window. My head was still pounding, so I turned my phone off and laid my head back, as the flight lifted off the ground, and we ascended into the friendly skies.

I stepped away from the rental car counter, tucking the paperwork into my bag and walked over to the car as the attendant pulled it up to the curb. He handed me the keys and I hopped in and pulled off. I set the address to the studio into my navigation and followed the turn-by-turn directions. I spotted a Jamaican restaurant and decided to stop and grab some food, I ordered two oxtail dinners with rice and peas, plantains, with banana bread and some sodas. Candie was always super hungry in the studio, so I figured if I was going to pop up on her ass, I could at least feed her. We hadn't texted or talked all day, which wasn't uncommon for us, but I knew she was in her feelings, so I shot her a quick, *I love you* text to test her temperature. After about five minutes, she still hadn't responded so I knew that she was giving me the cold shoulder. One thing I could say is when her ass wanted to ignore a nigga, she would act as if you didn't even exist. I shook my head and laughed at her stubborn ass. I would play her game for now, but she was going to play mine tonight.

I pulled into the parking lot of the address that I was given, grabbed the food bags and hopped out. I walked into the front door and checked the board, looking to see where suite K was located. I walked towards the elevator but was stopped by security. "Excuse me, sir, which suite are you headed to?" the scrawny guard asked. I looked her over and chuckled to myself because if somebody really wanted to do something, this nigga wasn't going to do anything about it. She looked to be about a buck-five soaking wet.

"Suite K, Royalty Records, session for Candie Monroe," I said politely. She looked over her clipboard, took my name, directed me to the suite, and bid me a good evening.

I stood outside the door for a second as I listened to Candie's voice boom over the speakers. Damn, my baby sounded good as hell, and she was living her dreams. She had come so far and I was proud of her. I honestly felt like an asshole; I had been treating her shitty the past couple of months, but I planned to make it up to her while I was out here, if she would give me a break. I walked into the studio and all eyes were on me, but I was scanning the studio, wondering why it was a million fucking niggas in this bitch. This is why I didn't like this shit, traveling all over the damn country with a million niggas always around, being all thirsty and shit over some pussy that they would never even smell. I looked at Jamie, and she looked like a deer caught in headlights. I nodded to her and took a seat on the couch closer to the booth, watching as Candie followed Jamie's eyes and we stared at each other.

Candie rolled her eyes and took the earphones from over her ears. "Trav, can we take a break? I'm starving and we been going strong for hours," she said into the mic.

"It's all good, boo, we can take a thirty," he said, standing up and walking out of the door. I looked around the room, and the rest of the niggas got up and walked out as well.

Candie stepped out of the booth with a mug on her face; she was sexy as fuck, even with an attitude. "Why the fuck are you here, Caine?" she asked, as she sat down next to me, and I handed her food to her.

"Damn, I can't pop up on my bitch? You got something to hide; you fucking one of them sucka ass niggas that was just in here?" I asked, opening my food and digging in.

Candie looked at me and then rolled her eyes as she opened her food. "Oh now I'm your bitch? If you came all the way out here to start some shit, then you could have stayed your black ass in Oakland. Why must you come and piss on my parade every chance that you get? I'm out here working, Caine, unlike you, I'm not out here fucking everything moving," she said angrily. "Maybe if you focused more on your craft rather than your dick, you could get further."

I let that comment slide because I knew she was pissed, but those low blows really fucked with a nigga's ego. I just shook my head. "I ain't come to argue, babe, I really just miss you and I'm not feeling the way things have been going with us. I figured maybe if we were outside of our normal element, then maybe we can get back right," I said, staring at the side of her face as she tried her best to avoid eye contact with me. "Plus daddy needs to feel his pussy," I said.

She looked at me with lust in her eyes and I knew she needed to feel me, just as bad as I needed to feel her.

I looked at my watch and saw it was a quarter after seven in the evening. "What time is your session over?" I asked, taking a large swig from my soda.

"We're damn near done, so maybe another hour at the most. Why, what you got planned?" she asked, looking at me quizzically.

I shrugged my shoulders. "Whatever you want to do, babe, I just want to be with you," I said. I couldn't front; I missed her ass like crazy. I missed that smooth comfortable feeling with her, things lately had been so tense and tonight, I wanted to get back to us. We finished our food and everybody began to come back in. I sat back and watched as Candie put the final touches on the song that she had just laid. Once she was done, she told Jamie that she would be staying with me tonight and after that, we were out. We walked to the car, holding hands, and just enjoying each other's touch. I told myself that I needed to do better, because I didn't want to lose my bitch.

Candie and I decided to stay in the room for the night. We had already eaten and were both feeling lazy; besides, Candie had an early session tomorrow. I wasn't a soft ass nigga, but I knew how to make my bitch happy, I had texted Jamie a list of things I needed her to grab, and I was waiting for her to hit me and let me know that she was downstairs. I looked over at Candie as she sat on the edge of the bed, removing her boots and socks. It was November and cold as hell in Oakland, but it wasn't as bad out here. Don't get me wrong, it was still cold, but not like the Bay. I watched as she pulled the socks off her petite feet. Candie was small, but carried herself big. She was 5'3" with a slender build; her hair was thick and curly, but she kept it short. Currently, it was tapered on the sides and thick and curly on top. Candie's skin was the color of mocha, and was soft as if she bathed in butter. I was a big fan of her plump thighs, they weren't thick, but they were well defined, and nicely proportioned to her small butt. Her breasts were ample and perky. I was rocking up just watching her as she undressed; I missed this girl. We used to be so close, so in love and inseparable, and that's what I wanted back. Shit, it's what I needed back.

"You going to stand there and stare at me all night, or are you going to come over and get what you're lusting over?" Candie asked, as she stood up and removed her jeans. I stood and watched as she seductively wiggled them down to her ankles. Once they dropped to the floor, she reached around and unfastened her bra, letting it fall to the floor with the rest of her clothing. I stared at her breasts as I watched her nipples harden.

"Get on the bed and play with it for daddy," I said, keeping my place at the door and watching her with lust in my eyes.

I was trying to get Candie to the edge of ecstasy, but I wasn't about to touch her until Jamie dropped off my package. Once I touched her, I was about to go in on that pussy. Candie removed her panties and lay back on the bed. With her knees pulled up and legs spread, she used two fingers and began rubbing her clit. I watched as she started to get wet; her pussy was glistening from the stimulation, and I couldn't wait to dive in that creamy shit. Candie moaned and threw her head back as she pleasured herself; I loved to watch her make herself come. Watching her sex faces was a huge turn on, not only because she was pretty as hell, but also because I knew that while she was pleasing herself, she was thinking of me. It boosted my ego to know that just the thought of me could make her climax.

Candie opened her eyes as she dipped her fingers inside; she stared at me as she dipped her fingers in and pulled them out, placing them into her mouth. "Come play with me, bae," she said, enticing me with her eyes.

"Not yet, make my pussy come and then I got you later," I said, as I watched her bring herself to a climax. After she came, she just lay there lazily; I walked over to her and kissed her deeply. "I love you, Candie Girl."

She looked up at me and gave me a half smile. "I love you more, Caine," she said and closed her eyes.

"You better and you got me fucked up with all of them dumb ass posts you be making all on social media. Your ass going to keep up playing with me like you ain't got no nigga, and you going to find yourself with my foot up your ass," I said seriously. Candie giggled lightly, but I wasn't playing with her ass. I sat there staring at her ass, as she lay there with her eyes closed. I hope she didn't think that she was about to take her ass to sleep, because I had something to wake that shit right on up. I sat up as I felt my phone vibrate; I looked at the screen and saw that Jamie was finally downstairs. "I'm about to run and grab some ice, bae, I'll be right back. Wake that ass up," I said, getting up and going downstairs to meet Jamie.

I walked into the hotel lobby and saw Jamie standing by the bar texting on her phone. "What's up, Jamie?" I said, as she looked up smiling hard.

"Hey you," she said, handing me a shot of Patrón. I grabbed the shot and threw it back as I looked around the lobby at the patrons that were scattered around. "So when can I get some time? Niggas been playing me to the left lately, and I know it's not because of Candie," she said, with a slight attitude.

I shook my head at her ass; this was typical female shit. I had slipped up and fucked Jamie a few times on some drunk shit. Now her ass felt that she could call on me whenever, and blackmail me if I didn't come and break her off when she wanted it. I know it's not slipping if you keep falling into the same twat, but I had to keep telling myself that I had slipped up, because on some real shit, Candie would be devastated if she ever found out.

"Man… Jamie, cut it out ma. I'm here with my broad, trying to get us back on track and you down here sweating a nigga, over some dick that doesn't even belong to you. Get the fuck outta here. I appreciate you for bringing me the shit, but kick back, ma," I said, grabbing the bag off the bar.

Jamie glared at me for a second and then licked her lips. "Whatever Cocaine, when you get bored with that old pussy like you always do, you better hope I'm still keeping it warm for you," she said with a wink, before I turned away and went back up to the room to my girl.

I swear, I get myself into the dumbest of situations. I walked back into the room and went to work, grabbing the items out the bag and preparing my perfect night. I walked into the room and Candie was knocked out. That was cool though, because it gave me time to set up, but after that, I was going to wake her ass right up. I walked into the bathroom lighting the aromatherapy candles and placing the chocolate-covered strawberries on the side of the tub. I turned on the water in the large tub and adjusted it to a comfortable temperature, before adding bubbles and lavender bath salts.

Once everything was set up, I went back in the room to wake Candie up. She was looking so peaceful, I almost didn't want to wake her, but this was our night to spend some quality time. "Bae, wake up," I said, kissing her on the nape of her neck; she stirred a little but didn't wake up. "Candie girl, wake up, baby," I said a little louder this time, while licking her ear, This time, she opened her eyes and smiled; I held my hand out and she took it. I pulled her naked body up and led her into the bathroom, where her bath was awaiting.

"Aaw baby, this is nice, you trying to get some cutty tonight huh?" she asked, with a slight smile.

I laughed and shook my head. "Hell nah, if I just wanted pussy, I wouldn't have to do all of this to get it. I mean, that's my shit. I just wanted to make you feel good and show you that I'm sorry for being an asshole lately," I said, as I helped her step into the tub. I turned out the lights and let the candles illuminate the space. I walked out and went to grab the bottle of Belaire Rosé and two glasses. Once I returned to the bathroom, I stripped out of my clothes and climbed in the tub. Candie scooted up some to give me room to slide in behind her. Once I had sat all the way down, she adjusted herself between my legs, leaning her head back onto my chest.

For a moment, we just sat there in silence, lost in our own thoughts. I had been doing Candie wrong lately and I really just wanted to get back on track. I had let my ego and my own insecurities get in the way of treating my woman right. Instead of handling shit like a man and telling Candie how I felt, I stepped out on her repeatedly, because I was in my feelings. Candie was my heart and it felt as if every day I was losing not just my bitch, but also my best friend. I treated my broken ego with new pussy, forbidden pussy, drunk pussy, all of that. I just prayed that we got it together and none of my skeletons came out the closet. I leaned back and started putting my words together. When Candie and I would spend quiet nights at home, we used to freestyle for each other. I would rap to her how I felt, and she would sing back to me. This was how we expressed ourselves, and I wanted to bring that feeling back.

I get caught up sometimes and forget that you're human, like pleasing me is the only thing you supposed to be doing/I let my ego speak for me when I should just speak from the heart/But I'm a hood nigga girl, sometimes I don't know where to start...

I was so into telling her how I was feeling that it seemed I was rapping for twenty minutes when it really had probably only been about three. Once I was done, I felt as if a weight had been lifted off my shoulders, I sat and waited for Candie to start, but she never did. I leaned up to look at her and she had tears streaming down her face. "What's wrong baby?" I asked, tilting her head so that I could look into her face.

"This shit isn't healthy, Caine. We fight, walk out on each other, and you go off and disappear for days, with no phone calls, texts and no explanation, like that's cool. You can say all these fancy words and rhymes, but it doesn't make up for the disrespect you show me day after day, fucking other bitches and not being there when I need you most." I could tell that the shit she was speaking was hurting the hell out of her, because some of the words were running into each other, and some I couldn't understand. I caressed the side of her face and wiped the tears that fell freely.

I didn't have anything to say, so I remained quiet. So many secrets were lingering in the shadows, and I didn't want to sit here and lie to her at this moment. I just wanted to feel what we had been missing. "I love you, Candie; know that, if you don't know anything else," I said and gulped down my glass of champagne.

"Love can't fix everything, sometimes you have to let something else be the reason," Candie said, as she got up and stepped out the tub.

I shook my head, because I had a feeling that this was just the calm before the storm. I stood up as well and stepped out of the tub, letting the water out and blowing out the candles. Candie turned on the light and hopped in the shower; I was tempted to hop in with her, but I left her to herself. This night wasn't exactly going how I wanted it to.

Chapter 5: Candie

I climbed in the bed with a heavy heart. I thought that this night was going to be chill and smooth, but it was anything but that. I appreciated the effort that Caine had made to come out here and apologize, but I wanted to see action. I was tired of the same ass "I love you and I'm sorry" speeches. Those words could never repair the emotional damage that he has caused, and to know that his disrespect was fueled off his ego was outrageous to me. I lay in bed naked, my mind wandering; maybe it was time to move on. Staying in an unhealthy relationship would keep my heart content, because Caine was the man I loved, but it wouldn't keep me happy.

After a couple of minutes, I felt the bed dip and I could feel Caine getting underneath the covers with me. I welcomed his body heat, even though I was mad and hurt; it was as if my body craved for him. I had to feel him, so I turned over and faced him with my eyes closed. I wanted to feel him, but I didn't want to look at him or talk to him; I just wanted to inhale his presence.

Caine slid down in the bed and spread my legs, lifting them over his shoulders. I relaxed my body and prepared to let go of my frustrations. I could feel Caine's warm breath tickling the flesh between my thighs, and my body tingled in anticipation of his lips connecting with my body. I closed my eyes as I felt his tongue tease my inner thigh; his mouth was so close to my hot pocket, I was ready to grab his head and smother him in it. However, I would let him get to it and not rush. "Get that shit, bae," I said, just as he dove in tongue first into my wetness.

Caine's mouth was like heaven. Shit, he talked enough shit with it, so it better had been worth something in the bedroom. I arched my back as Caine's tongue twisted and twirled inside of my pussy as if he was trying to scoop out the last of his dessert. My eyes rolled to the back of my head; it felt like Caine was sucking the soul out of my body through my vagina. "Babe!" I moaned aloud, as I tried to scoot away, but Caine locked his arms around my thighs and pulled me back towards him. I locked my hands around his wrists and rode the wave while he locked his lips around my pearl tongue; I inhaled sharply at the way his lips were shooting electric currents through my body. "Fuck, bae…" I said as I felt myself about to cum.

Caine was sucking on my clit and slipped two fingers inside my dripping wet opening. I normally didn't like to be fingered, but the way he was eating my shit had me ready to stick a finger in my damn self.

Caine twisted his fingers around and around as he sucked even more aggressively; the faster he went, the more I could feel my orgasm build up. I thrust my hips in his face and in seconds, I was cumming all over his mouth and nose.

My body was shaking as he stared in my eyes and came back up, releasing his manhood from his boxers. He had me feeling so good, I couldn't move or talk. I forgot just how good he could make me feel and now that he had reminded me, my mind was making me rethink all of the emotions I was going through. Good sex could make that shit happen, but I knew better than to forget all the things that had broken my heart. Caine placed his left arm above my shoulder and balanced himself, guiding himself inside my walls. He didn't have the longest piece of equipment, but the width alone was tantalizing. When he entered me, I grinded my hips into him and squeezed my muscles, gripping his dick. Caine and I got lost in the rhythm of our bodies, as we sexed each other all through the night in every imaginable position.

The next morning, I woke up with an ache between my legs that I hadn't felt in a while. I smiled to myself as I got up to prepare for my day. I gathered my things and hopped into the shower; I had a photo shoot at eleven and was due back in the studio by five that evening. It was only eight, but I needed to get back to my hotel, where my things were. I had at the shoot location an hour before, to ensure that we could get a proper start on makeup, hair, and wardrobe. All of this was exciting, because it was different from planning your own video shoot as an independent artist. Under the label everything was so extra it was like there was a person for everything. I texted Cass and Dezi last night and sent for them, so they should be here later on tonight. I was in L.A. working, but what fun was it to be out here and it's just all work and no play? I mean Jamie was here with me and we were super cool, but it wasn't like having my besties.

Once I stepped out of the shower, I stood over the sink, drying my hair with a towel. I stared in the mirror, pleased that my face was clear of blemishes and breakouts this morning. Fewer blemishes meant less makeup; I hated makeup. I liked the simple stuff, such as lipstick and eye shadow; anything else was definitely for special occasions. I grabbed the pack of toothbrushes off the sink and opened it, pulling out a pink one. Placing a glob of toothpaste on it, I started brushing my teeth, humming the melody to the song I was planning to record later on today. I had been working hard, writing these new songs, and trying to make sure that my debut album would be everything I dreamed of. Being a break out artist, it was imperative that my first single and first album be different, and something that will have everybody wondering what was next to come from me. I would be meeting with a couple of writers later on this week, and I was excited to be working with two of them. Juelz Lee was a great writer that had worked with some very big names, and Jianni was a very talented writer, nominated for various awards over the past few years. I was so juiced to get the chance to work with them on my first album that I could barely contain myself.

I was so lost in my thoughts; I didn't even feel Caine walk up behind me, until his morning wood was sitting between my ass cheeks. I looked into his eyes and looked away as he eyed me lustfully. I shook my head at his nasty ass. "Back up Caine, I'm on a tight schedule and fucking with you, I'm going to be late," I said, as I took a step up towards the sink. Caine tried ignoring me and licked my neck, before sucking on it with slight pressure. I pushed him away from me. "Caine stop... I have a photo shoot today, stop trying to leave your hater marks on me."

Caine sucked his teeth. "Damn, you sure know how to suck the fun out of some shit," he said, kissing my cheek and walking towards the toilet to pee.

I glanced at him, wondering if I could make time for a quickie, but I know that if we got started, we would most definitely turn it into a full out session. One thing that Caine had never been was quick; I wasn't trying to be fucking up over his ass and he wasn't even acting right. Caine thought I didn't hear his damn phone chiming all damn night from Facebook and text messages. I didn't reward bad behavior; I may have let him fuck my brains out last night but this morning, I was back to business.

I walked back into the room and threw on the Nike jogging suit that Jamie had brought for me to change into for the morning. Even though Caine was my boyfriend, it was still embarrassing doing the walk of shame in the same shit I walked in the hotel with. I didn't have any panties on, but after last night's love session, I didn't mind.

"What's up lil mama, you ready to do it moving?" Caine asked, carrying his duffle bag over his arm.

I looked at him and scrunched up my face. "I thought you were staying until tomorrow?" I said, eyeing him suspiciously. Yesterday when he showed up at the studio he'd said that he was staying two days.

"I was, but now I'm leaving later tonight," he said, as we walked out the hotel room.

"Clearly Caine, that ain't telling me why though. You came out here, popping all that slick shit about wanting to be with me and spend time. Now soon as you come to make sure I ain't got no niggas in my face, and you came and left your mark on my pussy, now you ready to hop on the next plane back to Oakland!" I said angrily, snaking my neck and rolling my eyes. I didn't even know why I was getting so damn mad; shit, I have work to do and Dezi and Cass will be here later. I shouldn't have given two fucks about him leaving, but at the end of the day, this was my nigga. Of course, I would feel some type of way about it.

The problem in relationships was that niggas always tried to make you feel bad or stupid when your intuition kicked in. This nigga thought he was slick but I wasn't even about to sweat the small shit, niggas would come and rain on your parade and make sure that you weren't doing shit just so they could play you to the left and go do what they want. I wasn't even with the shit today.

"Come on Candie, you already know that it ain't like that. I just had an artist book a session and she's paying like fifteen hundred man... beats, time, and mixing. I'm not passing up no dough. Shit, you want me to sit up under you like a bitch, while you out here getting your check. I'm supposed to miss money, because you in your feelings on some insecure shit, my nigga you tripping." Caine always got hella defensive when he was up to some shit, trying to make it seem like I was trying to be clingy and shit, when I was just wondering what made him switch his plans. The nigga act as if I asked him to come out here, when he's the one who hopped his ugly ass on a plane. Once we were in the car, I pulled out my phone to check emails. I wasn't about to let Caine ruin my damn mood.

"I don't know why you over there pouting and shit, you act like I'm leaving this very second. I'm still about to spend all damn day with your ass, damn!" he said, slamming his fist into the steering wheel.

I turned to face him, puzzled because I hadn't said shit and I damn for sure didn't have a damn attitude.

"Nigga you getting real mad over some shit that I never said, who the fuck do you see pouting? I just don't have the time for your fucking games and I chose to stay silent so as not to ruin my damn mood. Now you can take that fake ass nutty you trying to throw, and hand it to whatever bitch you running back to Oakland for, because I'm not for it today!" I yelled, with my hand all in his face.

This nigga had me all the way fucked up, I swear he was bipolar and three parts retarded, because he just didn't get it. I was going to call that nigga's mama and see if she had ever had him tested for crazy, because we could for sure use an extra check in the house. I shook my head and stared out the window as we pulled up to my hotel. Once Caine threw the car in park, I jumped out and walked briskly through the lobby. Jamie was already on her way to the set, so now I was stuck riding with the retard. I used my key to enter my suite and grabbed my bag of cosmetics, along with a couple of clothing items. I really didn't need anything because they were going to hook me up, but I still liked to have some things of my own. I was in and out in less than ten minutes and rushed back outside, so that we could get there quickly.

As soon as I opened the car door, Caine was ending his call, and I rolled my eyes at his ass. I couldn't stand his black ass and now that he was out here acting like his normal self, I couldn't wait for him to hop on the plane, get back to the Town so that I could be rid of his bad vibes. We rode to the set in silence; the only sound in the car was the voice from the navigation and I didn't even mind. Caine knew that I didn't like to listen to music on days when I had a lot to do. I liked to focus on my music and get my mind right to get in my zone. I looked around as we arrived on the set; from the outside, it looked like a large warehouse. I got out, grabbed my bag and purse, and walked around the car towards the door.

Once I got to the door, Caine grabbed my bag off my arm and pulled the door open for me, moving to the side to let me walk in first. I walked down the small hallway and looked for the unit that I was assigned to. Once I reached it, I could hear voices and it sounded like there were a million people inside. I took a deep breath, because I already knew that I was about to walk into a whirlwind of madness. Once I entered into the large space, Jamie snatched me up and pulled me into a back room, where I sat down for hair and makeup.

While I was getting my hair and makeup done, I was introduced to a million different people: wardrobe, directors, photographers, models, dieticians, and personal trainers. My head was spinning with all of the people coming in and out; the director had run down the theme of the shoot, and his vision. I was feeling his ideas and was ready to get in front of the camera and show out. Once I was done getting my face and hair slayed, I went straight to wardrobe to get dressed for my first look. I was loving the pieces that they had picked out, because they were definitely within my comfort level. I just knew they were going to try to throw me up in some flowery, poofy, fringy shit, but I'm figuring Jamie made sure to check the pieces before I arrived. My first look was a black bustier with a pair of low-rise black leather pants and some sexy fire engine red boots. Once I was dressed I was on set and in front of the camera.

I was posing and vibing to the music blasting from the speakers; I was really feeling myself on set and used this time to let loose. The photographer was cool and sexy as hell; his name was Cree. I'm sure that helped put me in my element. Everything about his ass was sexy; he was tall, solid, and caramel-colored, with light eyes and a nice beard to bring them out. However, the thing that really set me off was his voice. That deep baritone had me creaming all in my panties. After about an hour of straight shooting, he called for a break, which would give me time to change, get a touch up, and grab a small snack.

I walked towards the refreshment table to see what was there, and almost jumped for joy when I saw a nice pot of chicken and corn chowder. I loved that shit; I swear I only came across it on settings such as these. Once I grabbed a small bowl and water, I walked to the back of the studio towards the hair and make-up room. On my way there, I passed Jamie and Caine; Jamie's ass was smiling ear to ear as she and Caine talked. My stomach did a flip as I watched them interact, but I brushed it off. They were looking rather comfortable, but I could have been tweaking, because of how Caine had me feeling right then. Either way, I had other shit to worry about.

I walked right past them as I ate my chowder and sat down, waiting for the makeup artist to do her thing. I must have been hungry as hell, because I had scarfed that shit down in record time. Christina grabbed her brushes and went in on my face, while Jay added tracks to the top of my hair. They made my curls bigger and bouncier, and it added some golden color into my look. I closed my eyes as Christina added color to my eyelids.

"You all smiles and flirting with the photographer, like you trying to fuck that nigga. It's bad enough you got your titties all out, but do you got to seduce blood too?" Caine whispered in my ear.

I rolled my eyes. "Caine, get the fuck away from me talking all that dumb shit. I ain't did shit but what I'm supposed to do and unlike you, I would never disrespect you that way," I said, highly irritated with his nonsense. I don't know why this nigga felt the need to always come and piss in my damn cereal.

Caine walked away and I got up and went over to get dressed into my next look. I looked over as Caine was talking to Cree; he looked up and eyed me with a scowl on his face. I turned my nose up at his ass and flipped him the bird. "Bitch," I said under my breath.

Soon as I turned around, I noticed Jamie staring in their direction, with lust in her eyes. I stared at both of them for a moment and hoped for her sake that those googly eyes were for Cree and not my nigga. I never had any thought before that she was attracted to Caine, but I wouldn't put anything past anybody. I had known Jamie forever, so I prayed that she wasn't flawed, because I would hate to have to fuck their asses up. I decided to push that shit to the back of my brain and get back on set. The rest of the shoot went through effortlessly. Caine's dumb ass continued to shoot daggers and occasionally came over trying to run shit, but I ignored his ass and did my thing. The images were amazing and I couldn't wait to meet with my team, so that we could agree on the album cover photo.

After the shoot, we rushed over to the studio, we were pushing it on time and I didn't want to be late. I walked into the studio and shook hands with Avery, who was in charge of my development team. "Hey Candie! How are you liking L.A.? Jamie said that you were looking for a condo out here. I can have my realtor hook you up with some fly shit if you want," she said as she was looking through her phone. I looked over at Caine and watched as his jaw flexed. I hadn't mentioned that I wanted to move out here, but at the end of the day, if I'm trying to move on with my life, then I wasn't obligated to tell him shit.

"Yeah, shoot me that number later on," I said, setting my stuff down on the couch behind the engineer's chair. I spoke to Trav, the same engineer that I worked with last night; he was real cool and chill, and so far, had all my shit sounding very crisp. Avery introduced me to *the* Juelz Lee, which was the writer that I was working with today; I was too juiced to be working with him. Once Avery had introduced me and

Jamie to the team we jumped into the first song, I had written the song the other day and the instrumental was produced by a cool established producer from the Bay.

I was really feeling good about this track; it was called "Let Me Breathe" and the vocals on it were crazy. I stepped into the booth and waited for Trav to load up the track. I looked through my phone and saw that Cass had texted me to let me know that they had just checked into their room and would be here shortly. I was hype; we hadn't kicked it in a minute and I was ready to turn the fuck up, but first business. I looked at my watch and realized it was about to be a long ass night; it was only six and we were scheduled here until at least midnight. I pulled up the notepad on my phone and looked for the words to the song. I hummed the melody and tried to find my key; I glanced up and saw Caine smiling all into his phone. I wanted to know who the fuck he was texting, but I needed to just focus on my shit and get these damn songs done.

We had rocked out and finished "Let Me Breathe", along with another song called, "Lifted". Now I was sitting with Juelz and we were going over a new track called, "Come for Me". Juelz had popped open a bottle of Rosé and we were chilling; I looked up just as Cass and Dezi walked in. I jumped out of my seat as soon as my besties walked through the door. "Aye, shout out my bitches!" I sang as I gave them both hugs. I looked up and saw that Cass had brought her friend, Rob, and his brother, Jimmy. I spoke to both of them and went back to my seat, so that I could hurry up and knock out the rest of these tracks, and then we could hit the city. I threw myself into these songs and sung my heart out in the booth. I was really feeling all the tracks on this album, and I couldn't wait to show the world what I had been working on. I stepped out of the booth hot as hell, I grabbed a cup of Rémy and took a sip, as I swayed to the beat and sang the lyrics to the last song that I had laid down. *"You can let me be the one to touch your heart, for a moment."* I was tipsy, but it was cool, because we were damn near done here; I was ready to get shit poppin'.

"Yaaaasss bitch, sing it, baby!" Dezi said, as she stood up, threw her arm around my shoulders, and began swaying with me.

I continued singing with the track as Trav laughed at our antics, while he was bouncing it to the hard drive, and saving it into my file, with the rest of the tracks that we had laid for my album.

We were in our own zone and feeling good, until Caine walked up to me and grabbed my arm. "What's up, bae?" I asked, with a slight smile. I was trying to be cool, because I knew that he was about to get on the plane and I didn't want us to leave each other on bad terms.

"Shit, let me holla at you real quick," he said, as he pulled me out of the studio. I reached back, grabbed my cup, and followed him into the hallway. Soon as we were standing in front of each other, I looked up at him and waited for him to talk. "So, now you about to be out here acting up with Cass and Dezi for the rest of the week?" he asked.

I looked up at him and rolled my eyes. "Caine, you know I damn near always send for Cass and Dezi when I go out of town. This time ain't no different, so what's really good, nigga?" I said, with my hand on my hip. This nigga always found something to bitch about and I wasn't beat for the bullshit today.

"What's really good is your mothafuckin' ass out here making plans to move out to fuckin' L.A.! How the fuck are you moving to another city, when you got a whole ass man in Oakland, a place to live and a whole ass life in Oakland? How you out here telling people that you looking for a place to live in Los Angeles? Bitch, how does that work?" he yelled, jumping in my face.

I backed up and placed my hand in the middle of his chest. "Nigga, don't get fly in this bitch because you in your feelings; we ain't been right for months, and your ass out here fucking on anything and everything in Oakland. You expect me to just sit around like it's cool? Nah nigga, I don't rock like that, you can keep that shit and have it in Oakland. I'm doing my thing and you still doing the same shit, you were doing five years ago, with no progression. The fuck I look like? You right; I got all of that shit in Oakland, but what the fuck is it doing for me?" I screamed back, heated. I was over the conversation and over arguing with Caine's hoe ass; he could get the hell out of my face and return to Oakland now.

I turned to walk away and Caine grabbed my arm. "Candie, don't walk away from me; this shit ain't something you just walk away from. So you ready to call it quits? Now you aren't coming home?"

I shook my head, because I didn't feel like dealing with this now. I didn't know what to do and I really didn't even know how to feel at the moment. The goods that we had together were great, but the bad was always the worst, so I had to take this time to figure out if the good actually outweighed the bad. "I will see you in a few days, Caine," I said, and walked away. I still had one more song to lay down and then we were out.

***

We walked into the bar and it was packed, I looked around and was ready to have some fun. I grabbed Dezi's hand and started grinding my ass on Cass, as I danced to K. Camp's "1Hunnid" song. We were loaded and I really needed to let loose, so that I could get my life together when I got back home, I had a lot to think about, but tonight was about partying. We walked up to the bar and ordered two rounds of Patrón; I looked up and scanned the room to see who was around. I guess it was just habit, I didn't live out here and didn't have any beef with anybody out here, but still I liked to know who was around me. Bitches were haters and niggas didn't know how to act sometimes. After feeling comfortable about my surroundings, we took our shots and then went to move around the club to get shit popping.

We went towards the upper level and found some seats; from the top, you could see the dance floor, the entrance and the bar. "Where are the guys?" I asked Cass.

She looked around and shrugged her shoulders. "I don't know Sway, I been with you remember?"

I nodded my head and stood up so that I was leaning over the banister. I looked down and spotted Cree, the photographer from my shoot earlier today. I smiled at the thought of his sexy ass and imagined what his muscular arms would feel like wrapped around me. I knew that I was wrong for even having thoughts about the next nigga, but I couldn't help it. He was just too damn good looking and it was hard not to think about him in other ways, especially when I was in his presence. After a few minutes, I spotted Rob and Jimmy walking up the steps to join us, they were both carrying bottles of Goose and accompanied by about four other guys. I laughed because they were so damn hood, but I fucked with them tough. They were from Oakland, but both lived in L.A. now, playing for different basketball teams. Rob played for the Lakers and Jimmy played for the Clippers; they had both just recently gotten signed and were coming into their first season.

Once the guys came upstairs, the party started for real; we had the upper level of the club smackin'. All the bitches were trying to make their way over to where we were. It was funny, because rats could smell cheese from a mile away, and these bitches must have smelled that money cologne radiating off of these niggas. They were definitely trying to get a taste of what they were serving. I looked around for Cass and Dezi, but they were both entertaining a couple of young rich niggas, so I decided to go make the trek to the restroom alone. I descended the stairs and pushed my way towards the restroom, looking around and admiring the ambiance of the bar. It was a hip-hop bar, but the crowd was very diverse and it seemed as the staff was great, and the DJ was definitely killing it.

I got to the restroom and the line was long as hell. I shook my head because I had to pee like a racehorse and I would probably be standing here for close to thirty minutes. Bitches always wanted to spend a million years in the bathroom. First, they walked in and looked in the mirror, fixed their hair and makeup, because they see how messed up it got while they were turning up and then they used bathroom. However, most of them were super drunk, so it was like their pee was never ending, and then they came out, washed their hands and fixed their hair and makeup again. They used another ten minutes so that they could take selfies and group pictures, and they did this all in a bathroom with only two stalls, but they went in with a crowd of about six.

After about five minutes, I was already over standing in line; I had to go and I was going now. I almost rushed the line, but when I looked over at the men's restroom, I realized that it was only one other guy in line. I stood in line and watched as he walked in and came out about a minute later; as soon as he exited, I went in. I had to go so bad I looked around and admired how clean their restroom was; it was nothing like the women's. I made a mental note to start using their restroom more often.

As soon as I finished handling my business, I walked over to the sink to wash my hands; I looked in the mirror and felt satisfied with my look. I looked towards the door as it opened and immediately felt embarrassed. Cree looked outside the door at the sign and then looked back at me; I gave him a slight smile as I grabbed a paper towel to dry my hands.

"Damn, I knew it was too good to be true," he said, shaking his head. I'd never even paid attention earlier to how many tattoos he had. That nigga was tatted up like a subway in Harlem and it made him even sexier to me; he was inked up from the neck down to his fingertips.

"What is too good to be true?" I asked, tilting my head to the side as I crossed my arms over my chest, as if I wasn't standing in the middle of the men's restroom.

"The fact that you are beautiful as hell, but you're a man," he said, shaking his head and walking towards the urinal with his back towards me. "Do you mind?" he said, over his shoulder.

"I'm not a man!" I yelled out, a little louder than I expected.

I covered my eyes and turned around as I realized that he was actually peeing in front of me. I couldn't actually see anything, but the thought alone had me feeling that we were both violating each other.

"So if you're not a man, then why are you in the men's bathroom?" he asked, turning around and walking over to the sink, where I was still standing.

"Do you see that line at the ladies room? I wasn't standing in that," I said, rolling my eyes.

Cree laughed, showing off his pearly whites and I admired his smile. That beard had me ready to jump on his ass right here, but I was in a committed relationship. Something about Cree had me wanting to break a few rules.

"Well, I'm glad you're not a man, because you had me ready to go fuck a few bitches tonight to remind myself that I was all man, and not in any way attracted to one," he said, winking and grabbing my hand as we left the restroom. Once we were in the hallway, I ran right smack into Dezi and Cass.

"Umm bitch what the hell did you just do, coming out of a public bathroom hand in hand with this nigga?" Cass asked, with a frown on her face.

"Well bitch, at least you chose a bad one," Dezi said, raising her hand for a high five.

I shook my head. "Excuse you, bitches, I was only coming to use the bathroom. The line was super long, so I used the men's, but this was my photographer from this morning, Cree. He just happened to walk in on my way out." I said, laughing.

"Hello ladies, your beautiful friend was just in there trying to convince me that she wasn't a man. I'm here to say she's all woman," he said, laughing and rubbing my cheek.

"Nigga you got me fucked up," I said, doubling over from laughter. "He don't mean it like that, we were just talking," I said as we all walked down the hallway back towards the main area.

Cass turned towards me and let me know that they were going to grab drinks from the bar and asked if I wanted anything. I told her to grab me a double shot of Don Julio. I knew they were just giving me time to talk to Cree and I didn't mind that at all.

"So, what's up, ma, your nigga must not be here tonight?" he asked.

I forgot all about Caine being at my shoot earlier. "No, he had to get back home, actually," I said, now feeling guilty for being all up in the next man's face when I had a man at home. I was being disrespectful to our relationship, so I needed to get the hell away from this sexy ass man, before I got myself into some shit that I couldn't get out of.

I smiled at Cree. "I really should—"

Cree nodded his head and cut me off. "It's all good, ma, I don't even peg you as the type to be doing ya' man dirty behind his back. It was nice seeing you again and great working with you today. You have a beautiful voice and maybe we will run into each other again," he said as he winked and passed me his card. Just like that, he walked off and left me standing there staring at his back. After a couple of seconds, I turned around and walked towards the bar to meet back up with my girls.

I walked up to the bar and Dezi turned to look at me. "Bitch, if you don't make him your side nigga, I will."

I laughed because her ass was crazy as hell. We grabbed our drinks, headed back upstairs and continued to party the night away. I looked at my phone and sent a text to Caine.

Me: *Thank you for coming to spend time with me bae, I know that we don't get along all the time but I honestly want to work through this and get back to us. I love you daddy.*

Caine: *I love you too, Candie Girl, you really mean the world to me and we will get this right.*

I put my phone away and glanced over my shoulder. Cree and I caught each other's eyes and I gave him a weak smile, before turning back around and swaying my hips to the music that was booming from the speakers.

Chapter 6: Caine

I lay back after texting Candie and placed my phone on the dresser. I instinctively ran my hand over my face as I looked down at the warm set of lips that were wrapped around my shaft. Man, a nigga couldn't get right for shit, but after the past couple of days with Candie, I had to release some frustrations. When I was having sex with Candie, I was making love to my pussy. I didn't want to hurt her; I wanted to be gentle and attentive to her, making sure that she got hers before I got mine. With these other bitches, I was straight disrespecting the pussy, no compassion and I couldn't care less if they came or not. My motto with these other hoes was, "you better get yours before I get mine, because I wasn't coming back for yours". I grabbed both sides of Jamie's head and started bobbing her head wildly in my lap. I know that I was out of pocket, but I really was trying to keep this crazy bitch from running back to Candie and telling her ass about our deception.

After I left the studio, I sat in my car for a while smoking and winding down time, before my flight was supposed to leave. I could have gone to the airport and waited, but I was contemplating whether I should just stay for the extra day, or get on the plane and go home and make this money. Candie's last comment had me feeling as if I was just some lame ass local nigga, and I wanted to prove to her that I was more than just that. As I was sitting there, I saw Jamie walking out to her car. I was hoping that she didn't notice me sitting there and would just go on about her business, but of course, I didn't have any such luck. Jamie walked over to me and we had a short conversation, mostly her talking trying to convince me to let her give me some head. She was so trifling that she had offered to hop in with me and suck me off right there in the parking lot, where anybody could walk out and catch us. I was good on all that; I turned Jamie down and told her I was cool and going to the airport. After she volunteered to send some screenshots of some texts we sent from a few weeks ago to Candie, I agreed to meet her back at her room, which was down the hall from Candie's.

I wasn't stupid; I knew that fucking with Jamie wasn't going to make anything better. The moment she wanted to go run back and spill the beans, I was done. I can't lie and say I wasn't attracted to Jamie though, the bitch had a body on her and she was good with her mouth. If she wasn't Candie's friend, I would probably keep her close, but she wasn't wrapped too tight. Jamie tightened her jaws and sucked the soul out of my dick. I couldn't do shit, but throw my head back and let her do her thing. I placed my hands out to the side as I felt my toes curl and my nut build up deep within my balls. A couple of seconds later, I grabbed her head and pushed myself deep into her mouth as I shot my load out, aiming at the back of her throat. "Shit!" I yelled out as she got up and straddled me.

"I want you to make love to me, baby," she said seductively, as she leaned in and tried to kiss me, I turned my head and sat up.

"Girl cut that shit out. Lift up and bend that shit over," I said, stroking my semi-erect manhood. I was just going to get some head and dip, but I figured that since I was already fucking up, I might as well fuck something.

Jamie stood to her feet and climbed on the bed on all fours; her ass was looking right in the pink lace panties that she had on. I grabbed the panties and snatched them off, ripping them right down the middle. I threw them across the floor and stroked myself as I rubbed the head around her wetness. Her shit was so wet that I was damn near slipped in, just playing with it.

"Damn ma." I said, hypnotized by her pretty ass sitting up high in the air. I swear the pussy was talking to me and I was ready to talk back. I placed my dick right at the front door and just sat it there, moving it in small circles. I reached over and grabbed the condom off the dresser, ripping it open. I held the condom for a moment as I let myself sit there for a second; I was just savoring the wetness before I dove in.

I rubbed the head up and down between her butt cheeks and stopped right at the opening of her waterfall, applying a little pressure. Jamie pushed her ass back at the same time and the head of my dick slipped in.

"Oh my God," she gasped, "Give it to me daddy."

I couldn't lie; I was stuck between a rock and a hard place, because I wanted to pull out and put this condom on, but I needed to feel her wetness with no filter for a little while longer. I placed the condom down on the bed next to her, and grabbed her hips as I pushed myself all the way in and held still for a moment. I threw my head back and bit my lip trying to stop my body from tingling. I rocked my hips side to side as I hit her walls from one side to the other; I pulled out to the tip and then rammed myself back into her, making her ass cheeks jiggle. I repeated that same stroke and smacked her ass hard with my hand, making her ass shake like a bowl of Jell-O.

After that, it was a wrap, I started slamming into her ass, trying to see if I could get my dick could come out through her mouth.

"Agh! Baby, you hitting my spot," she said, as she started throwing that shit right back at me. I swear, her shit heated up about another ten degrees and she was squeezing the hell out of my ass. I curled my toes and bent my legs, as I used the balls of my feet to control my balance. This was some good ass pussy and I was damn near ready to bust, but I wasn't ready to hop out of this shit just yet. I started hitting her with death strokes; I grabbed her weave and wrapped it around my knuckles. I placed my hand in the small of her back and put some extra pressure as I pumped in and out of her.

"Don't run now, take all this shit," I said, as sweat dripped off my brow onto her back. After a few more pumps and feeling her juices squirt onto my pubic hairs and balls, I was ready to let go. I gave her two hard pumps and pushed deep into her, as I felt my kids shoot out deep inside her.

I collapsed on her back and we lay there for a moment, breathing hard. "Fuck!" I said, knowing that I had just fucked up; it was already hard enough getting rid of Jamie, but now I had exposed her to unfiltered dope dick.

I hadn't had random sex that good in a minute, but I needed to get the hell away from Jamie's ass. I couldn't be giving her too much of this good shit, because it was liable to drive a bitch crazy. I hopped up quickly and walked to the bathroom, turned on the shower and hopped in, washing away my indiscretions in a rush so that I wouldn't miss my flight. I stepped out the bathroom with my towel pulled tight around my waist, while Jamie was lying across the bed, naked as the day she was born, staring up at me with sleepy eyes. Just seeing her lying there had awakened my dick once again. I shook my head and gave him a short squeeze to get him to act right. I couldn't go diving back inside that shit or I would never leave, and I had to get the hell out of there for more reasons than one.

"Go get a Plan B in the morning, Jamie, don't forget," I said, as I pulled on my clothes, grabbed my phone and bag from the side of the bed, and walked towards the door. I turned back around and Jamie had her eyes closed. I just prayed her crazy ass went and got that damn Plan B pill tomorrow.

***

I was sitting in the studio, working on a beat with these female artists that I had been hearing a lot about. They were super talented and had a cool little buzz in the Town; we were sitting in the lab vibing. They had a bottle of Avion as well as a bottle of Belaire Rosé. They were goofing around. talking shit back and forth to each other. I was really feeling their vibe, because even though they were hella goofy, they were definitely about their business. Most people come in the studio, book four hours and spend two hours writing, an hour and a half laying their verse and the rest of the time, trying to hustle me out of a beat. These two came in with four songs that they laid as soon as they stepped in, and now we still had an hour left of their session. I had pulled up some unfinished beats and was shooting them one free.

Josh walked in the door and looked around the studio, stopping when his eyes fell on the smaller girl that was sitting on the chair next to me. "Damn, what's up Ty baby?" he said, as she stood up and hugged him tight. They stared at each other for a moment with smiles on their faces. They must have forgotten that they weren't alone, because they were still standing there lost in their own world.

"Damn you niggas done lost your ability to speak?" I said, laughing at how goofy they looked right now; clearly there was some kind of chemistry between them, because their asses were running out tight now.

"Shut up nigga, this my boo right here and I ain't seen her in a minute. Her ass got a few hot singles and turned Hollywood on me," he said, as he slapped her on her ass. Ty giggled and sat back down; for the next two hours, we just chilled in the lab and got lost in the music.

After the ladies left the studio, Josh and I decided to go get some food. Candie would be coming back tomorrow afternoon, and I needed to talk to my bruh before she came home. I pulled into the parking lot of the steakhouse and Josh and I hopped out the car. I looked at my phone and pressed ignore; this bitch, Joy, had been blowing me up for days and I had already spoke my mind. Why she was still blowing me up was a mystery to me. We sat down at the table and both ordered a beer and a couple of shots of Hennessy.

Josh shook his head at me with a knowing look on his face. "Nigga, you stay in some shit. What bitch is that?" he asked, as I shook my head and rubbed my hands across my waves.

"Man, that bitch, Joy. I swear that hoe is psycho. Her ass called me the other day talking about she wants to talk, so I call her ass back. She on my damn phone talking about Christmas is coming up, and she wants to take holiday pictures and shit," I said, laughing. I still couldn't believe that her ass even had the audacity to say some shit like that. Shit, it was only the second week of November; we hadn't even gotten past Thanksgiving yet.

Josh started laughing with me. "Bruh, what the fuck? Then what you say?" he asked, looking up as the waiter came and placed down our drinks.

"My nigga I told that bitch straight up, what the hell I look like taking holiday pictures with you, and I won't even take an Instagram picture with your ass.

That bitch better go find her son's father and take pictures with him."

I threw my shot back and chased it with my beer; I swear, these hoes just didn't know how to stay in their place. Now her ass keeps texting me talking about just come and meet her tomorrow, when she goes to take her pictures with her son and she has a surprise for me. Honestly, I hadn't seen her ass in a few months and didn't plan on dealing with her crazy ass at all, but she said that meeting her would be beneficial. I guess I would go and see what the bitch had for me, and then dip on her ass.

Josh shook his head. "I'm amazed Candie hasn't killed your ass yet. I swear you can't keep your dick in your pants if your life depended on it, and in actuality it kind of does. Candie's ass is crazy and you going to set her off one good time and regret that shit," he said.

I nodded my head because he was right. Candie was real chill most of the time, but when she got mad, she turned into the offspring of Satan. Josh and I ate and drank for a couple of hours, before we decided to turn it in. I headed home, anticipating seeing my girl tomorrow when she came home. I had cancelled any studio time the next day, so that I could go and meet Joy, and then spend the rest of my day with Candie.

I lay in bed and made a mental list of things that I needed to change in order to get my life back on track. I knew that I had been wilding out over the past year and I needed to clean my life up and get my shit together. I needed to go and holla at my moms, because she could always get inside my hard ass head and put me back on the right track. I picked up my phone and scrolled to Candie's name, pressing the call button. I listened to the phone ring a few times before her voice came over the phone.

"Hello," she answered.

"What's up, bae, what you got up?" I asked, hearing a lot of commotion in the background as if she was out somewhere. I looked at the time and it was after midnight.

"Hey, shit, we're out having a late dinner at this nice little Italian spot. I think Jamie is drunk her ass keeps talking about how she's in love and some ol' other shit. I don't know what she's talking about, because her funny ass keeps talking about we all know who this mystery man is," Candie said, laughing aloud. I tensed up as I listened to Candie, who was obviously quite tipsy herself.

I prayed that Jamie's dumb ass didn't come out and spill the damn beans tonight. "Damn, that's hella crazy bae, y'all better not get too drunk. Where are Dezi and Cass and who is that nigga in the background?" I asked, feeling myself getting mad. I swear they better not have been out with no niggas.

Candie giggled. "Ssshh daddy, cut it out, that's the waiter talking to Rob and Jimmy," she said.

I stuck my hand in my shorts and adjusted myself, hearing Candie intoxicated and calling me daddy did something to me and I needed her to get home fast. I forgot about the threat of Jamie fucking up my relationship, as thoughts of being up under my bitch took over. I didn't have any issues with Rob and Jimmy being around, because they had been around Candie since I met her and had proven to be like brothers to the three girls.

"A'ight baby, I was just calling to hear your voice. I cancelled everything so that we could spend the day together tomorrow when you get back, so I will see you then," I said.

"Okay, I love you, Cocaine," she said, calling me by my nickname.

"I love you too, Candie Girl." I hung up the phone, placing it on the nightstand as I got comfortable and let sleep take over.

The next morning I woke up and got prepared to meet Joy at the picture studio. I parked next to her car and climbed out, eager to get this shit over with and get back home. I texted Joy, letting her know that I was outside. After a few minutes, she responded telling me to walk through the doors and come through the hall that led outdoors behind the building. I looked up at the photo studio and it looked like a large house, it had a nice little set up. I would have to check them out and use them for some of the artists that I worked with. Once I walked outside, I nodded my head. It was a large yard set up with a fake grassy area, a picket fence, and a sitting swing as well as a play structure, which were all props. I looked up and scrunched up my face in confusion as Joy made her way over to me. I felt anger take over my body as she approached me. I knew now that her ass was most definitely on bullshit.

"What the fuck is this Joy?" I asked, as I walked over to meet her halfway; we were standing in the middle of the grassy area and I couldn't believe what I was seeing.

"What? This? This is our baby, Caine. You didn't think that fucking without a condom would come without any consequences, did you?" she said sweetly, I let out a deep breath and shook my head; I swear that this was a psycho bitch.

"So what the fuck, Joy, you thought that you would keep it all a secret and then come to me like this, and I'm just supposed to what ... welcome the situation with open fucking arms?" I asked, raising my voice slightly as I took a step towards her.

"I've been trying to tell you this, Caine, but you been playing me to the left. Every time I call and try to see you, your ass always act like you too busy. Then you hit me the other day on some shit like you cool on me and don't want me calling your phone anymore. You want to play me for that black ass bitch and I'm carrying your seed? You got me fucked up Caine!" she yelled.

I crossed my arms and tried to calm down, before I seriously slapped this damn girl. "So now what, Joy, you think I'm going to just up and leave my girl because you said you're pregnant? It doesn't work like that, ma, it's not easy like that. We ain't have a relationship; what we had was sex and nothing more. No real dates, no commitment, not even any mutual friends, you don't know shit about me and I don't know shit about you," I said, as I lowered my voice so that we could have a civilized conversation. I had to watch what I said, because I didn't want to set her off to where she would run to go break the news to Candie, before I had figured out a way to tell her myself.

Joy shook her head and I could tell that she was trying to hold back tears, I walked up towards her and placed my hand on her shoulder and stared into her face. Joy was cute, high yellow with natural hair that she kept in long dreadlocks and her tips were dipped in blonde. She had a small waist, well, used to have a small waist, and a nice sized booty, but no titties. "So when are you due?" I asked as she placed my hand on her belly; she wasn't super big, but she was definitely showing.

"April twelfth I'm twenty weeks today and I have a doctor's appointment later today, can you come with me?" she asked.

I looked at her and thought about it, I had plans with Candie and her flight was scheduled to land in two hours. I shook my head and leaned in, placing my head against her forehead. "Yeah, I will come with you, Joy, but I ask that you give me time to figure this shit out. If that's my baby, then I will definitely be there to make sure that he or she is well taken care of," I said, rubbing her stomach again.

I didn't know how to feel, because I knew that this shit was far from what I needed now. Just when I was trying to cut her off, she hits me with this shit, I can't even lie; I was spooked. I knew that once Candie found out about this, she was going to go dumb on my ass and then she was definitely going to leave me. There was no way to get around it, I had cheated on my girl with this broad and now, she was having a baby. It's not as if we were broken up and I messed with Joy and she got pregnant. No, I crept off with the next bitch and ran up in her raw, and now this was the outcome. As much as I wanted to run off and say fuck all this shit, I was taught better than that and I planned on doing right by my seed, even if it meant I would lose everything I had. There was no way I would turn my back on my child.

I kicked back and watched as Joy and her son, Joey, finished the photo shoot, I scrolled through my social media and looked through Candie's page on Instagram. She looked as if she had enjoyed herself while she was out of town, because her pictures looked like she was happy and free of worry. I wondered how long she would keep that smile. I had done so much behind her back and I knew that once shit hit the fan, it would be a minute before it stopped flying. Once the shoot was over, I hopped in the car with Joy, leaving my car there in the parking lot so that I could ride with her to her doctor's appointment. I looked at my watch and saw that Candie's plane would be landing in a few minutes. I was glad that she had parked her car at Jamie's and told me that I didn't have to pick her up.

After the doctor's appointment, I was feeling like maybe I needed to take the time to get to know Joy better, I mean shit, we were definitely about to have a baby and we barely knew anything about each other. I had Joy pull up to my car and once she parked, we both hopped out; her son had fallen asleep in the back seat, so we stood outside the car to talk.

"So you're about to go home to your girlfriend?" Joy asked, with a somber look on her face. I felt bad that I had to leave her, but I knew that I had to get home to my girl. I leaned down and kissed Joy's lips; I don't even know what made me do that shit. I don't know if it was the fact that I had heard my seed's heartbeat and she was carrying my child or what, but I guess the combination of all of that had made me want to kiss her juicy lips.

"I can always come spend some time with you later on this week. We can go grab a bite to eat or something," I said. As she leaned back against the car, I watched as a tear slipped from her eye and I instantly felt bad. "Come on, ma, I will follow you home," I said helping her back into the driver's seat and once she was inside, I walked around to my own car and jumped in.

Once I pulled up to Joy's apartment, I bounced out my whip and opened the driver door, helping her out of the car; she opened the back door, but I told her to go open the door. I grabbed Joey out the back seat, walked into the house, and went to place him in his bed. I pulled the door closed, walked back out to the living room, and sat down on the couch. Joy came and sat down next to me, and I just stared at her for a moment.

"You want me to make you something to eat before you leave?" she asked.

I looked at the time and figured why not. Candie hadn't called yet, so I could kick back for the time being. Joy got up and handed me the remote control, before she walked into the kitchen. A few minutes later, she came back and brought me a beer and a bag of sunflower seeds. I looked at her for a moment, because maybe she did know a little bit about me. I loved to kick back and watch sports with a beer and a bag of seeds. "Thanks," I said, and she nodded and returned to the kitchen.

After about forty-five minutes, Joy came back into the living room with two plates in her hands. She set them both down and then walked away, coming back a few seconds later with two bottles of root beer. I bowed my head to say my grace and then picked my fork up; Joy had whipped up some grilled salmon, a salad, and fettuccini Alfredo with garlic bread. The food was so good, I didn't even know that she could throw down like that; while we ate, we talked about anything and everything. I told Joy about my childhood, how I started with music, and we talked about our five-year plans and shit like that. I learned about how Joy had been on her own since she was sixteen years old; she talked about her days hustling and her relationship with her son's father. Talking to her had put her in a different light, and I was very intrigued. We ended up putting on a movie, I rolled a blunt and took it to the face; about thirty minutes into the movie, we were both out like a light.

"Mommy, I'm hungry." I looked up as Joey stood in front of us. I sat up straight and looked around as Joy got up and pulled Joey towards the kitchen.

"Fuck!" I said, as I looked at my phone and saw that I had been sleep for three hours. I had about eight missed calls and hella text messages. Candie had text a few times, asking where I was and I knew that this night wasn't going to end well once I got home. I looked at a text from Jamie and shook my head; she was really starting to work my nerves. She had texted talking about I better not be out cheating on her and Candie, while I'm not answering my phone. This shit was for the birds; I put my phone away and got up to join Joy in the kitchen.

In the kitchen, Joy was plating some fish sticks, with the Alfredo and salad for her son; she poured a cup of juice and sat it down in front of him. I watched as she doted on her son lovingly and I fully respected it; I knew that I could trust her to raise my child right. I knew that I should have taken my black ass home, but I wasn't ready to kill my peace and deal with the consequences of my actions yet. I had promised Candie that today we could spend time together and work on our relationship, but I wasn't able to keep that promise, so I knew that I would be walking into a hostile environment. I made a decision to stay with Joy tonight and go home to Candie tomorrow; she was due back out of town later this week, so I knew that I would have to make up with her before that day comes. If I didn't, I was sure that she would make good on her attempt to leave Oakland and make L.A. her new residence. I wasn't going to let that happen at least not without a fight. The holidays were swiftly approaching and I needed at least to give her a Christmas that she wouldn't forget. At least she would have that before our world got shaken up.

Chapter 7: Candie

I sat on Honey's couch, eating a tub of ice cream; I was filling her in on everything that had gone down while I was L.A. It felt good spending time with my sister, because I really didn't get much time with her. Between my schedule and hers we were always missing each other. "So what's the plan for the holidays?" she asked.

I pushed a spoonful of ice cream in my mouth and thought on it. "I don't know, I'm really not in the holiday spirit this year, but if y'all really stuck on doing the family thing, I will do Christmas at my place. Then it's up to you and Sin to figure out who's doing New Year's," I said, as I placed another spoonful of ice cream in my mouth; I closed my eyes and savored the flavor.

"Why you not in the holiday spirit, sis?" Honey asked, looking at my quizzically.

I took a deep breath before I answered. "Bitch, now you know I'm never in the spirit, but I just got a lot going on and honestly, I have been thinking about moving to L.A. to be closer to the label. You know so I don't have to keep traveling every other week," I said. Honey had a deep frown on her face; I already knew that she wasn't going to be feeling that news, but I wanted to keep it real with her.

"Hold up, you got me fucked up. You are not moving to no damn Southern California, I don't give a damn what you and Caine are going through. Fuck him, you don't have to move away just to move on, what the hell will I do without you?" she asked, looking as if she was on the verge of tears.

"Honey, calm down, I'm not sure what I will do yet, but I'm at my wits end with Caine's ass. That nigga is unreliable, disrespectful, and he's just not what I need in my life. I have been loving him and riding for him since the very day that I met him, and now I realize that love can't always be the answer. Sometimes people have to work a little harder to make shit work. Love comes without effort; it's everything else that you have to add in and Caine isn't adding shit else. He thinks that he can say he loves me and it will make everything better," I said, with tears coming down my eyes. I hated crying; that shit made me feel weak and used, and I knew that I was neither of those.

I told my sister how fucked up Caine and I had been for the past few months, and she said exactly what Sincere had said; it was time for us to take a break. At first, I was convinced that I did not want a break, but now as I thought on it maybe we should just take a break, not an official break up, but just time apart to see what we really wanted. They say you never miss something until it's gone, so maybe we should see where being apart led us. I was just hoping that whoever "they" were, was going somewhere with that saying.

I looked at Honey and she had a look of pity on her face, but I didn't want her to pity me. I was a strong, educated, black woman that had been all over the world, doing what I love. I was talented, beautiful, and I had never let anything or anybody hold me back from achieving my dreams so there was nothing for anybody to pity. Caine was just a man, who bleeds, breathes and hurts, just as I do, so he could never break me; all he could do is make me a better woman for the next man, if he chose to let me go.

"Sister, you already know that I'm here and I'm going to always rock with you, no matter what. I fuck with Caine, but that nigga been faulty as fuck lately. I been hearing his name linked to a few different bitches and that shit right there ain't cool at all. I know a nigga will be a nigga, but at the end of the day, you can't be out here being messy as fuck and reckless because once that shit is coming back and meeting you at your front door, then you fucking up my nigga," Honey, said aggressively.

That was one thing about my sister and I; we were super protective of each other, I wouldn't let anybody fuck with her and her feisty ass wouldn't let anybody fuck with me. Honey would help me jump Caine, before she would let him out right play me.

I was pissed that Caine had flaked on me today, but I really had enjoyed spending time with my sister. I always spent time with my besties and Sincere, but Honey was fresh out of school and she was doing her residency at UCSF Children's Hospital. By the time she had a day off, she was spending it in bed, because she was so tired, but I supported my sister and I was very proud of her for her accomplishments. I checked my phone again to see if I had a text or missed call from Caine, and my phone hadn't done shit. I shrugged it off and just chalked it up; shit, he had to go home and deal with me eventually, so I wasn't about to continue stressing or lose any sleep behind this nigga. I hopped on my Instagram then checked through my follow requests and smiled when I saw that I had received a request from Cree. I swear he was so persistent, but I wasn't sure if that was a good thing or a bad thing. Sometimes niggas were persistent and then turned into a stalker. It's cute in the beginning when you're being chased and feeling like the nigga really trying to fuck with you, and then you realize that he wants to control you. I accepted his request, but I would just keep this shit on social media for now. Cree could most definitely cause some trouble, good trouble for my sanity, but trouble nonetheless, especially if Caine got a whiff of it.

For the rest of the night, my sister and I just kicked back; we talked about guys, our future kids and then did a ton of planning for the upcoming holidays. None of us had any kids, so I wanted to do something fun for Christmas and New Year's, because I knew that come this time next year, somebody will have popped out a baby. Cree had sent me a DM later in the night and we had ended up messaging until the wee hours of the morning. On one hand, he had helped to keep me from blowing up Caine's phone with rude ass messages and death threats. On the other hand, every time he made me smile or laugh, it made me sad, because I didn't want anybody but Caine to make me smile, or be able to evoke any kind of emotion out of me. I could sike myself out and say that I wasn't going to worry about Caine or hit him at all, but when your feelings are invested into a man, that shit sounds good for about the first hour. Once it starts to get later and the night turns into early morning, you lose all of that self-control and then anger sets in. You get to texting a nigga shit that you probably don't mean, but you are definitely feeling at that moment. You even start saying anything to get a rise out of their ass, by bringing up their mama and dead uncle, even their cross-eyed auntie; whatever it takes to get his ass at least to say fuck you.

I woke up the next morning, tired as hell. Honey had already taken off early this morning, before I had even fallen asleep, to make it to her shift at the hospital. I went into the bathroom to handle my hygiene and then walked to the kitchen to see what was good to eat. I opened the fridge and didn't see anything that I was feeling, so I put on my shoes, grabbed my things, and headed out the door. I would stop at the grocery store on my way home so that I could cook breakfast in my own kitchen. I had a taste for steak and eggs, with potatoes and wheat toast with apricot jam. Yes, I was about to fuck it up. I was in and out of the grocery store in less than thirty minutes and pulling up at home. I looked around and Caine's car was nowhere in sight. "Oh well, more for me," I said aloud, laughing to myself, because I knew that even if he was at home, I wouldn't have cooked his bitch ass anything.

I walked into the kitchen and dropped my things down. I took the steak out and seasoned it, placing it into a Ziploc bag and sitting it inside the refrigerator for the time being. I peeled the potatoes, placed them in some water, grabbed a bottle of Andre, and placed it into the freezer. I grabbed my phone and purse, and then went into my room so that I could take a shower; I turned on the water and lit a candle, dimming the lights in the bathroom. One thing I absolutely loved about my house was the dimmer in the master bedroom and bathroom; sometimes I just wanted to relax. I lit the vanilla candles in the room and stepped out of my clothing; it was an ugly day outside, so I would spend my day in the house writing and afterwards, I would find a good book to read. I stepped inside the shower and attempted to wash away all of my stress away. I didn't want to sit and the house and feel down, so I was washing away everything now, because I vowed not shed another tear today. I let the tears flow freely as I sang in the shower. I was feeling that new song by Rick Ross and Breezy called "Sorry". I lathered my washrag, scrubbed my body, and sang the words to the song.

I try to change, but I'm always out fucking around in the club.

Sorry don't make it right, I knooow.

I try to change but they always around pulling me down in bed, gave you my word but they were just broken promises, broken condoms, lipstick marks and unprotected sex.

I feel like shit, you know I ain't shit.

Sorry won't turn back the clock, baby I took you back cus' I knew you.

Wouldn't believe so I used you, I'm sorry. Sorry don't make it right.

I sang the words, thinking about my own life and wondering if Caine was ever really truly sorry for the things that he did. It was crazy, because too many niggas just chalked up the shit that they did as them just being a typical nigga, but when would they just take responsibility for their actions, instead of using that as their scapegoat? Sorry didn't make it right, actions did, and every day, Caine's actions proved that he wasn't truly apologetic for his mistakes. I stepped out the shower stomach rumbling. I skipped the lotion, found my Victoria's Secret onesie with the butt flap, and threw it on. It was cold as hell outside, and I planned to be nice and cozy inside for the rest of the day. I walked into the kitchen and pulled pans, grease, and utensils out and got to work. Once I finished cooking, I heard the front door open, I looked at the clock on the stove and it read 10:17 a.m. I shook my head and sat down at the table, pulling out my tablet and pulling up The Westbrooks show. I cut into my steak and placed a piece in my mouth. I closed my eyes as I savored the flavor, "Damn I'm good," I said as I continued stuffing my face and staring at the screen of my tablet.

I heard Caine walking into the kitchen, but I didn't pay him any mind. I didn't have shit to say to him, so I continued to do what I was doing.

"Damn, it smells good as fuck in here," Caine said, as he opened the stove. He closed the stove and then walked to the microwave, opening it and then closing it as well; he then walked over to the refrigerator and looked inside, closing it back. I held in my chuckle and kept my eyes glued to the screen as I continued to place forkful after forkful into my mouth. It was amazing how this nigga faked on me, with not as much as a call or text, and then had the nerve to come in here, expecting to have a plate put up. Tuh, this nigga was clearly smoking something good. Caine turned to me and I kept my eyes glued to the screen still. I wanted to look up and see his facial expression so bad, but I knew I would burst out laughing. "So you didn't make none for daddy?" he asked, as he sat down at the table like I invited him to join me.

"Not today, Satan," I said under my breath, taking my eyes off the screen to look up at him. I pressed pause on my show, preparing for the drama. "Why would I make you breakfast, Caine, did you wake up here? Did you call or text, yesterday, last night, or even this morning? Thanks, you can excuse yourself," I said, rolling my eyes and pressing play. I refused to let this retarded mothafucka' ruin my chill day.

"I'm sorry baby. I got caught up taking care of some shit. I've been trying to make some moves, you know Christmas is coming and I'm trying to make sure the money straight so I can get you everything you want," he had the nerve to say.

I pressed pause again. "Caine, I didn't ask you anything, didn't ask you where you were or what the fuck you were doing, so don't volunteer a lie that I didn't even ask for. Save that shit, because I don't care. Shit, Christmas is next week, so if you ain't got it together yet, just fuck it," I said, staring him dead in his face. I scraped the last bite onto my fork and placed it in my mouth, still holding his gaze.

I shook my head and got up to wash the dishes as I made my dishwater, Caine was still seated at the table, and I didn't plan on saying anything else to him. I thought of that old school song by Monica and DMX and wondered if that's really how niggas were when they didn't come home. I started singing Monica's part and tears fell from my eyes as I sang it loud,

So why you keep on holding on when, I'm right here, all you need is call

Don't be afraid, cus' she won't know at all...

You ain't gotta go home tonight, you can stay right here with me.

Don't you worry 'bout a thing, you're here with me.

I didn't understand how a nigga could have a woman at home and yet still be so weak for another bitch to where she had enough control to make him not come home. I shook my head and continued to wash the dishes.

Once I was done I turned around and Caine was still sitting there with his head in his hands. "Fuck you over there crying for? Nigga, don't act like you give a fuck now!" I said angrily, as I walked out of the kitchen. I heard Caine jump up out of his seat and follow behind me.

"On some real shit, Candie, I'm not in the mood for your slick ass mouth today. I've had a long few days and if you can't shut the fuck up, I will leave again," he said, getting in my face.

I turned up my lip at his statement. "You promise?" I asked throwing up the deuces, as if I cared if he left. "Nigga, that's what I want you to do, leave so I can enjoy my damn day."

I sat down on the couch, tucking my feet up under me and grabbing the throw blanket from the back of the couch, spreading it over my legs. I turned on my 50" smart TV and started my show back up from there. Caine walked back into the kitchen and I could hear him fumbling around with dishes. I didn't understand how he had probably spent all night and morning with a bitch, and didn't get breakfast. Please believe, if I spend the night away from home and the person I'm supposed to be committed to, the nigga better feed my ass before I cut. Niggas were dumb; I shook my head and focused on my show.

After a few minutes, Caine came in, sat down on the couch next to me with his plate, and started watching TV with me. I rolled my eyes. He didn't even watch reality shows. "Ain't that the little bitch from Instagram?" he asked.

I ignored him; I was told if I didn't have anything nice to say then don't say anything at all. I was mad, feelings hurt. and I just needed a moment because everything out my mouth was bound to be rude and sarcastic. For the next two hours, we sat watching episode after episode until I was caught up. Caine attempted to hold a conversation by making side remarks every couple of minutes, but I never responded, just as he never responded to my calls or texts. Shit, he could talk to whoever was blowing up his damn phone, his phone was vibrating off the hook and he was ignoring it. I was dying to find out who was blowing his shit up, but I don't even think I want to know.

I walked into the kitchen, grabbed my phone and saw that I had quite a few notifications. I laughed aloud when I noticed that Caine had gone through my phone. There were like three messages that moved up to drafts, so I knew that he had been all in my shit. I don't even understand why he felt like he had the right to go through my shit, when I didn't go through his. I had a few messages from my brother and sister, some from

Dezi, and one from Jamie. I looked at the text again from Jamie and decided to call her instead of texting.

"What's up, Jamie?" I asked, trying to figure out why the fuck she was inquiring about my nigga.

"Hey Choc, I was trying to see if you were with Caine. I know somebody that was trying to book some studio time and I was trying to see if he was available today for a four-hour session," she said.

I walked back into the living room and Caine was kicked back with his feet up, smoking a blunt.

"Caine, Jamie's on the phone," I said.

His eyes shifted a bit before he sat up and looked at me. "What's up?" he asked.

"She wants to know if you have room for a four-hour session today for somebody looking to do some work," I said, with my hand on my hip.

"Nah, tell Jamie I'm spending time with you today; they can book some time for tomorrow."

I rolled my eyes at how now he wanted to spend time with me, niggas were always a day late and a dollar short. I relayed the message to Jamie, but she didn't let up.

"Well can you tell him that they are on a deadline and really need to book today?" She asked.

I rolled my eyes because I know she just heard me say he said no.

"Jamie, I've been gone for a week and my nigga clearly just said no. All the damn studios in Oakland, you can't book them time elsewhere?" I asked snidely.

"My bad, Choc, I was just trying to keep the money in the family. These some ATL niggas and you the one always talking about Caine only being a local factor. I was trying to help y'all out and keep the money in the family."

Caine was staring at me as I stood in front of him with the phone up to my ear.

I shook my head. Jamie had been on some funny shit lately and I planned on calling her out on that shit, because no matter how long we've known each other, she worked for me and it was always business first. So whatever she had going on, she would want to separate it from what we had going on, because I was not about to let whatever attitude she had interfere with my money. I had three back-to-back road dates coming up and I was not about to deal with her attitude. She'd better get some dick before Wednesday came, because I needed her on her A-game. "Well thanks, Jamie, but he said not today," I said, hanging up, and throwing my phone on the couch before flopping down and looking over at Caine. "The fuck your ugly ass looking at?" I asked.

"You know you rude as fuck right? It's good though, I got something for all of that slick talk." Caine stood up and grabbed me. Throwing me over his shoulder, he was poking my sides. I wiggled, trying to get loose. I was not trying to be on good terms with his ass, but I hated how he knew the ways to break me down.

"Put me down, Caine!" I yelled, giggling as he nibbled on the back of my thigh as he carried me to our bedroom. "Stop Cocaine! We not friends, nigga." I said, still trying to wiggle out of his embrace with no such luck.

Once we were in our bedroom Caine threw me down on the bed and climbed on top of me, staring me in my eyes. I looked back for a second and then turned away. "Look at me Candie Girl," he said sternly.

I turned back slowly and stared into his handsome face. I didn't want to be mad or hurt, shit; I just wanted my nigga, the man that I loved to act right and treat me like somebody. It was one thing to take some shit every now and then, but it was another thing to continue to accept disrespect and cheating over and fucking over again. I closed my eyes as Caine started kissing me below my jaw line.

Somebody real is hard to find, somebody worth all your time.

Somebody who could tell you the truth, someone who loves you for you,

Someone who knows all of your flaws and doesn't impose try to control them let's you be free doesn't deceive give you the chance to believe, believe in some things.

Is that too much? I been on a search and I'm losing my hope

Is that too much, is that too much? I'm just trying to find love in a world so cold.

Is that too much? I just want an answer I can't be the only one.

Is that too much? Ain't gotta be perfect just give me a purpose to love.

I just want somebody body to treat me like somebody body

Don't be like everybody body all you gotta do is love me for me babe...

I sang into Caine's ear as he lay there sucking on my neck. I didn't know how else to open up to Caine with words sometimes. I used music to express my feelings because that was how we connected, when I sang to him I always sang from my heart and soul. When I talked most of the time, I knew that my words probably fell on deaf ears, but when I gave Caine the raw part of my heart that was when he understood me the best. I opened my eyes and looked at Caine sure that he heard me, he nodded his head and lay on his back, pulling me on top of him. "If you can't take care of my heart Caine, then just let me go. It's unfair to keep me around, knowing that you are going to continue to use and abuse my heart and take my love and forgiveness for granted," I said, staring into his face as he unzipped my onesie and released my body from the clothing.

"I know, babe, I promise to do better. I can't keep playing with you and expecting you to forgive a nigga every time, I'm ready to settle down and shit. A nigga ain't getting any younger and we gon' get this right, Candie, I promise. Just keep rocking with me like you have been and I won't let you down," he said as he kissed my lips passionately.

I nodded my head. "I love you, Cocaine." I slid off him and down on my knees, as I closed my mouth around his stiffness and began to suck slow and sensual, I let my tongue swirl around the shaft as I went down, and let my lips sit at the base of his dick, brushing against his balls.

We made a bond from the very beginning

I found my homie and my bestfriend

I'm a be there for you til' the very end

No matter what, no matter what, no matter what

We broke the rules we took it further in

We made a promise to each other we gon' never end

She gon' be there for the kid, no matter what

No matter what, no matter what

I slipped him out of my mouth and looked up at Caine with a smirk on my face. "You cheating nigga, you can't win quoting Future. I was expecting some real Cocaine fire," I said, laughing and placing his manhood back into my warm mouth.

I began to please my man as if it was my last job on Earth. I didn't rush it; I took my time and made sure to give him all that I had. I sucked him until he bust and didn't let up even after his seed shot down my throat. Once I was sure that he had released everything, I stood up and licked my lips. Caine grabbed me by my waist and pulled me down on top of him. I lifted my hips and mounted him; I sat down and took a second before I made a move. I began to rock my hips slowly and tighten my muscles around his thickness. I closed my eyes and threw my head back as I fell into a nice rhythm. Caine grabbed my hips and thrust his hips up at me as we fell into a slow grind making love as if it was the last time.

Caine scooted towards the edge of the bed and sat up, placing his hands under my thighs lifting me, causing a slow and steady motion. I closed my eyes as I felt myself reaching my climax. "Ugh, fuck me daddy," I moaned as I placed my hands on his shoulders, sinking my fingers into his flesh. The feeling of our bodies together had me wetter than the Pacific. Caine sped up and bent his knees as he stepped away from the bed; he began to slam me down on his dick. He was giving me pure dope dick and I couldn't do shit but accept it. I was moaning loud as hell as his thick rod continued to pump in and out of me, I could feel that familiar tingle, as my orgasm got closer. "I'm about to, fuck babe, I'm about to come!" I yelled out.

"Me too baby, hold on. Come with daddy," he said, as he started pumping harder and harder; soon as I began to release, I felt Caine cumming as well. I squeezed my muscles and wrapped my arms around his neck as we collapsed on to the bed. I lay there trying to catch my breath as I listened to the beat of our hearts in the silence.

After my breathing had returned to normal, I climbed off Caine and walked into the bathroom, grabbing a washrag. I turned on the water and waited for it to get hot before I grabbed a bar of soap and made a thick lather, before I walked back into the room and began to wash Caine up. After I was satisfied that he was clean enough, I walked back into the bathroom to rinse and went back once more to wipe him up, once he was all clean, I turned on the shower and hopped in for a quick wash up. I could not take a hoe bath for shit, it always made me feel so incomplete. I was in and out of the shower in ten minutes and returned to the room, where Caine was sitting on the edge of the bed looking through his phone with a frown on his face.

"What got you over there mugging?" I asked, as he looked up obviously angry; he shook his head and stood to his feet.

"Man Josh just text me, I sent two packs off the other day and they both got intercepted," he said, a little louder than he probably meant to. "I got to go meet up with Josh and figure some shit out, I can't keep taking losses like this."

I nodded my head, Caine and Josh sent off packages of weed out of state damn near weekly, so I knew that he would have to go meet with Josh, if they didn't make it to their destination.

"What time will you be back?" I asked, as I looked through my drawer for some panties and a bra to throw on. I know I said that I was staying in for the rest of the day, but if Caine was about to leave, then I was going to cut too. That session had given me a boost of energy and it was early enough in the evening to go do some shopping and then make it back into the house before it got too late.

Caine walked up behind me, and wrapped his arms around my waist. "I'm not sure, babe, but as soon as I'm done, I will be right back here with you. I need to hop back in my pussy before the night is over." I smiled as he licked my earlobe. I grabbed a matching black lace set and pulled it on. I then grabbed a pair of light blue Levi's and threw them on, along with a black cami tee and some socks. "Hold up, where the hell you think you going with your little ass?" he asked as he looked at me with his brow raised.

I looked up laughing at the face he was making. "Nigga, calm down. I'm about to finish up on my Christmas shopping. Dezi and I are about to blast to the city and hit the mall, if you don't mind," I said, grabbing a pair of knee-high leather boots and slipping them on. I stood up on my tiptoes and leaned into Caine for a kiss.

"Yeah okay, Candie, you better keep them niggas out your face," he said, smacking me on my ass.

"You got it daddy," I said. Caine walked to the dresser and pulled a black t-shirt out, throwing it on with a pair of dark Indigo 504 Levi's and some black and white 11's. We both grabbed a coat; after I sprayed on some Valentina perfume, I grabbed my purse, phone, and keys; we both hopped into our separate cars and peeled off. Caine honked his horn at me and I honked back, headed into the opposite direction.

I pulled up to the curb outside of Dezi's apartment and put my truck in park; I turned off the engine and stepped out, looking around to see who was outside. Dezi stayed in the hood, she lived right on 88th and Birch in the middle of all the action. I walked up to her door and I could hear her music blasting. I knocked and waited for a second. I knocked again, because I knew that her ass most likely didn't hear me the first time. After a few seconds, she still hadn't come to the door. I pulled my phone from my back pocket and called her number while banging on her door. After a second, the music was turned down and I heard her yelling, "Who is it?" she yelled getting closer to the door.

"Ya daddy," I said as I placed my hand over the peephole so she couldn't see who it was. The door swung open and Dezi had a frown on her face.

"Bitch you almost got ignored; you know I don't answer my door for nobody unless I already know they coming," she said, with her back turned.

"Hoe shut up you the one text me, talking about let's go shopping," I said, as I grabbed a canned soda out of her refrigerator and popped it open.

Dezi swung around and looked at me as if I was crazy, "Bitch that was like four hours ago and you never even replied. What if I had found another best friend to go with? Then what you would have done?" she said laughing.

I laughed with her. "My bad boo I had to get my issue one time, and knock it off; you only got one other best friend and that bitch is at work, so you would have been sitting right here waiting on daddy like you were," I said, blowing her a kiss.

"You make me sick." Dezi turned and grabbed her shoes and jacket, throwing them on, before turning everything off and walking towards the front door. I sat there looking down at my phone as I messaged Cree back; he had hit me earlier when I was still at home. "Bitch, you can get left, bring your ass," Dezi said, with her head cocked to the side. I laughed because her ass was always talking shit. That's why she and Cass were my besties because those two never let up.

"Here I come, hoe, watch ya' mouth," I said as we walked out the house.

Dezi locked up and we walked to the curb and hopped into my truck. Dezi hooked her phone up to my Bluetooth and started playing music from her phone. I scrunched up my nose at the Gucci Mane song playing; I reached over and turned the music down. "Umm bitch, you know I don't listen to no damn Guwop, try again," I said, as I pulled onto Highway 580 and headed towards San Francisco.

Dezi and I rapped and sang to the music the whole way to the mall, as we sipped on a bottle of Hennessy that she had pulled from her purse. I swear her ass was ghetto as hell, but I didn't mind, because if she hadn't had some drink already, I would have stopped at the liquor store myself. I hated going to the mall sober, especially this time of year when the malls were packed. Thanksgiving had flown by and I barely remember it; Christmas would be here in a week. Once we pulled up to Westfield Mall, I pulled to the curb to valet park. I didn't feel like searching for a garage that wasn't full and then looking for a parking space for this wide ass truck.

"Ooh bitch, you fancy, we see who getting money," Dezi said, imitating the nigga off the movie *State Property*. I laughed and handed the valet my keys and took the ticket as we stepped onto the curb and entered the mall. "So what's up with you and Cocaine Cowboy? I'm assuming that y'all good, since you let him all up in the pussy," Dezi said as we looked around and then stepped on the escalator, headed upstairs straight to Victoria's Secret; that was always our first stop.

I shrugged my shoulders. "We cool for now, but we will see, I got a funny feeling that some bullshit about to pop off, so I hope you riding with me when it do, bitch. You already know what kind of bullshit Caine's ass brings," I said. Dezi nodded, as we stepped off the escalator and headed into the direction of the large store that was bound to take a good chunk of my change today. I was getting all the females' gift cards for Christmas and I would grab myself some shit as well. I looked up as I heard a familiar voice yell my name. I stopped mid-step and turned around as I looked into the face of my ex-boyfriend.

Malcolm was my boyfriend for three years before I met Caine, even after Caine, I had went out with him and fucked with him a few times. I hadn't seen him in months and it was bittersweet seeing him now. The last time we kicked it we hadn't left on good terms.

"Candie, what's good, ma?" he asked, leaning for a hug. I wrapped my arms around him as he squeezed my ass and kissed my neck. I stepped back and looked into his handsome face. Mal was 6'3" dark-skinned and on the lean side. His hair was cut low with a short ducktail in the back. I waved to his cousin, G, and smiled at Mal as he smiled back at me.

"Hey Mal, how are you?" I asked. "Shit, I'm good my nigga, what you been up to lady? I heard you signed a deal with Royalty and shit, that's a good look. I guess now that you big time, you don't got love for a nigga no more," he said, as he set the bags that he had in his hands down at his feet.

I shook my head and looked over at Dezi, who was now having a conversation with G. They had messed around a couple of times over the years, but it wasn't serious.

I tilted my head so that I was staring up at him. "Now you know I ain't about to switch up just because I signed a deal, I'm a real bitch, you should know that." Malcolm grabbed my hand and traced the lines in my palm with his finger.

"Is that right? Is you still fucking with that fake ass nigga? Or you finally got your head right and left that loser in the hood where you found him?" Mal asked. I twisted my mouth and just stared at him. I wasn't really trying to answer any questions that had to do with my relationship with Caine. Mal shook his head, already knowing the answer. "Damn C, you running out still fucking with that bum ass nigga, but shit I guess you will wake up one day. So are you fucking with me tonight or nah? I heard you back on the road this week so a nigga trying to get a little time G-O-D."

I smiled and thought about it for a second, Caine had promised to come right back home, but he always promised one thing or another and didn't keep his word. I shrugged my shoulders, "Damn nigga, how you know all my business?" I asked, taking a step back. Mal just winked at me with his cocky ass. I nodded my head, just accepting it. "Shit it's good, just hit me, and we can link up after Dezi and I finish shopping," I said.

"Well how I'm going to hit you when you changed your number on a nigga?"

I laughed forgetting that I changed my number because one of Caine's little side bitches wouldn't leave me alone. I grabbed his phone and put my number in it; Mal leaned down and kissed my lips. I kissed him back and threw up the peace sign as Dezi and I walked into Victoria's Secret.

"You and Mal always gonna be that couple that should have given it another chance," Dezi said, as she picked up a cute little powder pink nightie.

I shook my head. "Dez, you already know the shit I went through with Malcolm's crazy ass. Them Frisco niggas be nuts and we're better as friends; much better than we would have ever been in a relationship. I love Mal, but I could never go back down that road," I said, as I looked through some of the bras.

"Yeah, you're right, but you never had to deal with any other bitches, if anything, you were the playa," Dezi said.

I shook my head and chuckled at her statement. I thought back to Malcolm and me; we were good when we were partying and having fun, but he was selfish and controlling. No, I didn't have to deal with other bitches and the lies as I do with Caine, but I couldn't deal with his control issues. Malcolm had a horrible mean streak and when he got on that hype, we were dangerous together. We had come real close to killing each other one night after one of my shows and I knew I couldn't stay with him. At the time, I was three months pregnant and we had gotten into it behind a number in my phone. We fought and after we had left each other bloodied and bruised, he chased me on the freeway and in an attempt to get away, I swerved around a truck that made a lane change at the same time and we collided. That night I was ejected from my car and had lost my baby. I thanked God every day for sparing my life, but I could never go back to Malcolm after some shit like that. Love was a bitch, because it would cause you to accept some shit that you wouldn't normally go for, but it most definitely wasn't a reason to accept anything.

Dezi and I were moving through the mall like professional shoppers, we had hit about six stores and were balancing bags like crazy. I was tired and ready for some food. "A'ight, we are in and out of this damn Timb store, if I see another got damn register I will scream. So come on bitch," Dezi said, as we walked out the Levi store and into the Timberland store.

As we walked in, we were greeted by a sales associate. I was looking for the calf length boots for myself, and a pair that I had seen online for Sincere. I sat down to try on a pair of heeled boots and nearly kicked somebody. "Oops, I apologize," I said, as I realized I had nearly knocked over a pregnant lady. I was trying to push my foot into the boot so I hadn't looked up, but I realized that the girl was still standing there as if I didn't already apologize. It wasn't the damn club, so I know she wasn't tripping. I looked up and into her face. "Can I help you?" I asked, as she stared down at me; I threw my hand out and snaked my neck. I recognized the girl from somewhere but I wasn't sure where, she looked one last time and shook her head.

"Nah, my bad, I was lost in thought," she said as she walked away.

"Well that was weird," I said aloud.

Dezi walked up to me with her eyebrows scrunched up. "Umm, who was the pregnant bitch that was over here eyeing you?"

I started laughing because her ass didn't miss a beat, I could be halfway across the world, and Dez would call like, who's that bitch that bumped you.

I shrugged my shoulders. "Girl, I don't know that bitch, she was standing here like she knew me. Maybe she thought I was her baby's fahva," I said and we started cracking up laughing. I didn't tell her that the girl was familiar, but I engraved her face in my brain so that the next time I would be on point.

After we had grabbed all of our items, Dezi and I headed towards the register and paid for our merchandise. We grabbed all of our bags and headed back into the mall, so that we could get back to the car. As we were walking out the doors, I spotted the same bitch standing outside Aldo's with an ice cream cone, once again watching me and then it hit me. I handed the valet my ticket and he rushed off to get the car.

"Dez, stay right here, I'll be right back," I said, as I sat down my bags and walked back into the mall. I twisted my head from side to side looking around for the girl, but I didn't see her anywhere. I walked into Aldo's and looked around, but I still didn't see her, "Fuck!" I turned around and walked back outside, just as my truck was being pulled to the curb.

I grabbed my bags and loaded them all into the truck, before I hopped in and waited for Dezi to get in as well. "Bitch, so why I think that pregnant bitch is fucking on Caine," I said as I pulled off and headed towards a gas station.

"Wait sis, come again?" I then informed her of the incident at the restaurant when the girl approached me in the bathroom when I was having lunch with Sincere a few weeks back.

"So did she ever say that she was actually fucking him?" Dezi asked.

I shook my head. "No, she never really said anything at all, but I mean shit; you know when a bitch got some shit to say and she's just trying to figure out how to come about the shit."

Dezi nodded her head.

My intuition was in overdrive right now, because I had been feeling like some shit was up, but only time will tell.

I pulled into the gas station. "Dez, call G and see what's up with him and Mal, while I go pump," I said, as I hopped out and walked around the truck to the pump. I slid my card and released the nozzle, placing it into the gas tank. I stood there wondering how deep that girl's relationship was with my man. I wanted to call Caine and flash, asking hella questions and shit, but I decided to wait. The ball would drop eventually if there was something up, and if it did then I would be ready for it. Once my tank was filled, I replaced the gas cap and jumped back into my truck. I looked over at Dezi, who was smiling from ear to ear as she talked with G on the phone. I waited for her to hang up before I pulled off, I sat back and grabbed the bottle from the back seat and took a swig, passing it to Dezi. Once Dezi hung up and looked at me with a sneaky grin, I shook my head.

"Bitch, hit the bottle and where are we headed?" I asked as I started up the engine.

"Well, G said that we can just go back to his spot and do dinner and drinks there. You know, just on some chill shit."

I nodded my head, I wasn't tripping; I really didn't want to sit in a restaurant or a bar, so that was perfect.

Dezi typed the address into the GPS and we pulled off. For a second, I felt guilty; I thought about Caine and I immediately felt bad. I picked up my phone and called him; I waited for a few seconds and listened as the call rolled over to voicemail. I hung up and called again getting the same thing; once I hung up, I sent Caine a text telling him to call me. I shook my head because I knew that once Caine had left the house earlier, I wouldn't be hearing from him for the rest of the day. It was going on 9 p.m. and he hadn't hit me once.

"Bitch. Fuck Caine! We're already out here and you want to have second thoughts. Fuck that nigga, you better live your life, shit. I'm more than positive he don't be feeling guilty and calling your ass before he runs off with Keisha, Tisha, and Pam, so get ya' mind right and kick back. That nigga leaves you on sucker standby day after day, and you feeling bad for kicking it with a nigga that you still got love for. Fuck that," Dezi said, passing me the bottle back, I looked in my side mirror and switched lanes.

"It's not that easy though, sis, I'm not just loyal and faithful when he is giving it in return. I'm loyal and faithful, because that's what my heart tells me to be, but how long do you just let things go and continue to be loyal to someone that's not reciprocating the gesture?" I asked, shaking my head.

"Bitch I don't know, because you know that I ain't giving these niggas all of me, unless it's a ring on my finger. Laz and I are good together, shit, we're great together, but until he puts a ring on this bitch here then I'm still mackin'. You can't give husband treatment to a boyfriend, because then you give them no reason to marry you if you have given them all you have in a relationship where they have the choice to walk away." I nodded my head because that made a lot of sense. I had given Caine so much of me in these four years that if we were to break up, I wasn't sure if I would have anything left to give to the next man, and I didn't want to be that broken girl that couldn't trust a nigga because of the shit that my ex had put me through. "I'm not telling you to come here tonight and fuck Malcolm. I mean if you want to then do you, but just relax and have some fun, give Caine a taste of his own medicine. If he calls you before the night is up then kudos, but if not, then at least you were able to enjoy yourself as well."

I pulled up to G's house and parked in his driveway; I looked up and admired his home. G had been living nice since I had known him and had a few houses, but I had never been to this particular one. "This ol' balling ass nigga got up his Christmas lights like he trying to win a damn award or something," I said, as we walked up the stairs to the front door.

"Girl, you know he feels like he got to be one step ahead, always trying to be that nigga," Dezi said, as she rang the doorbell; we waited for a second before the door opened and Mal stepped to the side to let us in.

I walked through the door and Mal grabbed me around my waist. I turned and faced him looking into his eyes.

"I missed you, ma."

I nodded my head. "I know, nigga," I said as I leaned back to avoid the kiss that he tried to plant on my lips.

"Oh okay I see you want to play a few games tonight, bet I win."

I shook my head from side to side. "No games, Mal, but I just want to chill. We're not fucking tonight, let's just enjoy each other's company. Cool?" Mal nodded his head and placed a soft kiss on my forehead.

For the rest of the night we ate, drank and the others smoked. It was just like old times, I had texted and even called Caine a couple more times, but he had never responded, so I shrugged it off and swallowed a fuck it pill. I was beyond tipsy and didn't trust myself driving home, but I didn't want to stay here with Malcolm either. He had surprisingly been a perfect gentleman, but I wasn't sure how long that would last. Dezi and G had already snuck off to have some privacy and Mal was probably just as drunk as I was, so I knew he was sure to start getting a little more aggressive. I lay across the couch as I logged onto my Instagram. Cree had messaged me a few times, so I took the time to message him back, while Mal had gone to the bathroom. I was really feeling Cree; he was sexy, smart and had a way with words. We had been in contact every day since I came back from L.A., and I planned to see him when I got back in a few weeks.

"Still talking to multiple niggas I see," Mal said, as he leaned over the couch, staring down into my face. He grabbed my phone out of my hand and stared at the screen reading my messages with his nosey ass.

I shook my head. "Shut your ass up, I wasn't talking to multiple niggas then, and I'm not now either."

I knew that there was no way that Mal was going to ever let me live that down, but the past was the past and he needed to let that shit go, nobody was perfect and we all made mistakes. I forgave him for the shit that we went through, but I guess men never really forgave. Mal walked around the couch and straddled me. I took in a sharp breath because I hadn't been this close to him in ages and I wanted to be able to control myself, but I wasn't exactly sure if I could use my best judgment tonight.

"Let me get my pussy, C," Mal said, as he kissed my chin and then sucked on it.

I shook my head. "This isn't yours, Malcolm," I said, as I scooted down a little. I could feel him hardening against my pelvis and I didn't need any extra temptation.

"That's a lie, this will always be mine. Even if you marry that lame nigga that you love so much, my name will be written in stone all up and through this
136

pussy," he said, as he licked my lips and then kissed me passionately. I loved the feeling of his lips, so I kissed him back with no hesitation. I closed my eyes, because this was the beginning of a long pleasurable night. I knew that there was no running away now, so I pushed all thoughts of Caine out of my head and just let Mal take control.

***

I woke up feeling like I was being watched. I opened my eyes and Caine was sitting on the edge of the bed just staring at me. "What are you sitting there staring at me for? You about to kill me or something?" I asked as I rubbed my eyes and looked at the time.

It was only 7:00 A.M. and I was still tired as shit. I had to catch a flight to Washington later today and then I would be in New Mexico Thursday and Philly Friday and Saturday, then Sunday through Tuesday I was in Vegas, and then back home Wednesday just in time to get my house ready for Christmas on Friday. I was really going to need Caine's help while I was gone to get everything together so that by the time I got home I would just have to start cooking.

I looked at Caine, waiting for him to finally say something, but he was just sitting there like he had lost his words. We hadn't really said much to each other since the other day after I had spent the night with Malcolm, but we weren't necessarily fonking. I sat up in the bed and looked at his face. He was clearly upset, but why I didn't know.

"What's up babe?" I asked, pulling the covers up to my waist.

"I don't know, Candie, you tell me. Why the fuck that bitch ass nigga Malcolm texting your phone all through the fucking night for?"

I looked over to the nightstand for my phone and it wasn't there.

Caine pulled out my phone and started looking through it. "What you up to, Ma? Damn baby you sleep? It was good seeing you the other day, everything still candy, wink." He threw the phone into my lap.

I grabbed the phone and looked at the texts, shaking my head. "Why you even going through my phone, Caine? I don't go through your shit, so why you stay all up in mine?" I asked calmly.

Caine turned toward me and stared sternly in my face, but my expression didn't change. Yeah, I had kicked it with my ex nigga. Shit, I had even fucked Mal, but at the end of the day, I didn't even feel bad about it. Caine had been running around this mothafucka' for years just handing dick out for free, and I had still been sitting here like a dummy giving him chance after chance.

"Candie, I don't give a fuck about all that shit. Why the fuck is your ex nigga calling and texting your damn phone like it's cool? Did you fuck that nigga?" He yelled with fire in his eyes.

I shook my head and crossed my arms over my chest. "I saw him not too long ago and I guess he's feeling some type of way, and now he's hitting me. What else would you like me to say because that's all," I said as I got up and walked into the bathroom.

I didn't have time for his bullshit. Niggas always did their dirt, but didn't like that shit when it happened to them. It's never fun when the rabbit's got the gun.

When I came out of the bathroom Caine was gone, I picked up my phone and saw that he had sent me a text.

Caine: *You whack as fuck to still even be entertaining that bootsy ass nigga. All the shit that you said you went through and this nigga just texting and calling like you're not in a relationship. Fuck you, Candie, go ahead and hop on your plane and continue being a hoe. Bitch!*

I threw my phone across the bed and began to get dressed. I wasn't about to let Caine get to me. I wasn't about to cry over spilled milk and he could be mad, hurt or whatever, but shit, I had been all of those time and again so he would get over it eventually. I had things to do and I would deal with Caine later. Once I was dressed and fully packed up, I called Jamie and let her know that I was ready. I was going to leave my car and just have her come and swoop me up so we could head to the airport. I had a long week ahead of me and I just needed to get my mind right. I grabbed a scarf and wrapped it around my neck and then walked into the kitchen and made me a large thermos full of green tea with lemon and honey.

The weather was colder than it had been in years, and I needed to make sure that my voice was at top performance. I had seven days full of performances ahead and I couldn't come any less than my best. Just as I placed the cap on my thermos I heard a horn honk outside. I grabbed my bags and everything and took off out the door.

Chapter 8: Caine

"Aye, Josh, let me use your whip right fast, my shit getting detailed and I need to go pick some shit up," I said as I walked up the street to where Josh and Laz were smoking on a blunt.

"It's all good, bruh, don't crash my baby," He said as he threw me the keys to his Range truck.

I caught them out the air and walked up the block to his truck. I hopped in and started it up, peeling off the block to go meet my nigga, P. He had been holding a couple of stacks for me since yesterday and I was just getting time to come and grab it from him. I pulled up to the gas station and looked around to see if he was there yet, but I didn't see him. I grabbed my phone and got ready to call him, but he was pulling in as soon as I was about to press call. I popped the locks and hopped out of the truck then walked up to his passenger door and hopped in.

"What's up, brodie?" I asked, giving him dap as he passed me the stacks of money.

"Shit, you know I'm out here trying to make a dollar," he said.

"Fa sho', my nigga. I'll get at you in a week or so for the next round."

P nodded and I was out of his car and back in the truck just that quick.

I pulled off, and as soon as I hit the corner, another car swooped in front of me and cut me off, barely missing my bumper. The car was speeding up the block and that shit had pissed me off. I pressed my foot on the gas and sped up to the car. I pulled up on the side of the car and it was some young ass bitches behind the wheel, both of them had blunts and Styrofoam cups in their hands. I laid on the horn and swerved in front of them and then peeled off, leaving them in the dust. I hit the corner and soon as I did, 5-0 was right there. I hit the brakes and hit the next block, hoping that they hadn't seen me speeding. I looked into the rearview mirror and cursed under my breath at the red and blue lights behind me. I pulled over and shook my head, I had these stacks of money on my lap, so I grabbed them and put them in the glove box and grabbed the registration out in the process.

The officer walked up to my window and tapped on it lightly. I rolled the window down and nodded my head.

"Afternoon, sir, do you know how fast you were going in a residential area?" he asked.

I nodded my head. "Yes, I apologize, sir. I was in kind of a rush." I said as he asked for my license, registration and proof of insurance.

I handed him all three and he stepped away from the truck and walked back to his car. I waited for a couple of minutes for him to come back. I was getting impatient, but when I looked back at him in the rearview and he was walking back.

"Excuse me, sir, can you step out of the car, please?"

I looked at the officer like he was crazy. "For what?" I asked. "I mean, why do I need to get out of the car for speeding?"

I was getting mad, but trying to keep my tone in check. With the way the world was going, I didn't want to be another black man gunned down by the police for nothing. I stepped out of the car and the officer pat me down and then placed cuffs on me and sat me down in the back seat of the squad car, just as another squad car pulled up.

Now I was super confused because I didn't understand what was going on. The second officer walked over to the truck and they exchanged words and then began to search the car. I put my head back, irritated at the situation.

The first officer walked back to where I was seated and opened the door. "Sir, whose car is this that you are driving? Your license doesn't match the name on the insurance or the registration, and we found a few grams of marijuana along with a substantial amount of money."

I shook my head. "Fuck!" I said as I looked straight forward out of the window.

"So the car is not yours, sir? Are the items inside yours?" he asked.

I was pissed that I didn't think to look and make sure that Josh didn't have me riding dirty, but shit, it was done now. "Nah, it's mine. Can I have my girl come and get the car? I can't afford to have it towed. My girl is pregnant and needs to get around," I said, looking at the officer.

The officer stood silent for a minute and then nodded his head. He pulled me out of the car and then released the cuffs. When I turned around, he replaced the cuffs to the front of my body, then handed me my phone and let me make my phone call. I dialed Joy and prayed that she answered. Once she picked up I began talking.

"Hey, I need you to come down here to 9-0. I got pulled over can you come get the whip, please?" I asked. She let me know that she was on her way and I hung up.

I sat back in the squad car and waited for Joy to pull up. Once she arrived, the officer helped me out and gave me a couple of minutes with Joy. I told her to take Josh his keys and have him take her to pick up my car from around the corner and just hold onto it until I called her. I gave her a kiss on the cheek and then she pulled off, I was headed to jail for drug distribution, but I wasn't tripping because I wasn't on any paperwork, so I knew that I would be able to bail out.

Once I had gotten downtown and processed, I called Joy first and told her that I was cool and would call her once I was transferred to Santa Rita Jail. It was Monday, so I would most likely just wait until I went to court before I tried to bail out. My next call was to Candie, but I knew that she was busy so I wasn't sure if she would answer. She had been gone since last week, and this was her last day on the road. She would be coming home tomorrow and I know she was going to be tripping at the current situation. Shit, we already weren't on the best terms.

When Candie answered the phone I told her everything that had happened, leaving out the fact that I had Joy come and pick up my car. She didn't sound mad, but I felt bad because she did sound worried. We talked for a couple of minutes and I told her that I loved and missed her before we hung up. She was due back early tomorrow morning, so she promised to be at my court date. It was only days away from Christmas, so I needed all to go well. After I hung up with Candie, I made my last call to Josh just to buzz him in. Once I made sure that he would handle everything, I hung up and waited to be transferred to the county jail.

After another couple of hours just sitting and waiting, I was finally called and transferred to the jail. I didn't get processed until damn near three in the morning, and by the time I got into my bunk, I just wanted to sleep. I would be woken up early in the morning for court, even though I didn't have to be to court until the afternoon. I wasn't worried about the shit too much, but damn, the last place a nigga wanted to be was in jail. I was sure that even if they would try and make me sit for another court date, I would get bailed out, so I wasn't about to lose sleep over the small shit. I had Candie in my corner and I knew that she would make sure that everything was straight. I was hoping that Joy wasn't too stressed because this was minor shit. I had tried leaving Joy alone weeks ago, but once I found out that she was carrying a nigga's seed it changed a lot of shit. I had helped to create a life, and I wasn't going to make her deal with it alone, so I vowed to her and my child that I would be there from the very beginning. The situation was shady, but I couldn't wait until my seed got here.

The next morning, we were shuffled to breakfast and then shortly after transferred to court on the big blue and gold county bus. I saw a few niggas on the bus that I knew from around and we sat on there clowning and shooting the shit all the way to the courthouse. I sat for hours in the holding room awaiting my appearance; this jail shit was for the birds. I had a couple run-ins with the law a few times before, but I had been blessed to have never had to sit for anything longer than a few days.

Once my name was called, I was led into the courtroom and waited to address the judge. I looked around the courtroom, but I didn't see Candie. I shook my head as I saw Joy sitting toward the back staring at me.

"Fuck," I said under my breath. I wasn't expecting to see her there. Shit, I had never even told her retarded ass what time I went to court. The last time we talked, I had told her that I would call her after court, now she had me tripping because I needed to know where the hell Candie was. I just prayed that this bitch didn't do some dumb shit.

I was in front of the judge and back in the holding room in ten minutes. Just like I thought, they had scheduled another court date, and because the holiday was Thursday, it wasn't until late next week.

Once I got back to the jail, I hit the showers and went to dinner. I needed to get in touch with Candie and figure out what was up. Maybe her flight had been delayed and that's why she was a no show, but whatever the case, I wanted to check on her. I just prayed that her and Joy didn't have a run in at the courthouse.

After sitting in my cell for a little bit, I heard my door pop. I hopped up to see what was going on and the deputy let me know that I had made bail. I looked at the time and saw that it was just past 9 P.M. I grabbed my shit and bounced up out that bitch, nodding my head at a couple of niggas on my way out. I guess Candie was cool since I had made bail. I had missed her over these last few days, even though I was still low key pissed that she had been back in contact with her ex nigga.

I was pissed because I didn't see any reason for her ass to be in contact with no nigga that she used to fuck. If a nigga had it before then he would always think that it was good to get it, and it wasn't, so all of that keeping in contact shit was not flying with me. Shit, Candie had that nigga's name tatted at one point in time, they shared a child and hella shit, so call me insecure or whatever, but I really didn't want to hear shit when it came to her and that bitch ass nigga. I would beat her ass and his if I found out that they have fucked around since me and her been together.

I sat in the room with a few other niggas that were being processed out, thinking about my life and my relationship. I knew that I did my dirt, and a lot of it, but I couldn't deal with another nigga inside my bitch. That shit would kill a nigga's soul. Even though Joy was having my baby, she could do deal with whoever she wants to as long as she doesn't fuck him while she's carrying my seed. I cared about Joy because she was now the mother of my child, so I thought and cared about her well-being because my child's well-being was dependent on hers, but I didn't love her. I didn't care about any of the other bitches I dealt with and I didn't love anybody but Candie. I know I had a fucked up way of showing it, but shit, I did my best to let her know constantly that she had my heart. I took care of rent and bills and made sure didn't need or want for anything, even though she had her own money. But shit, I was going to do my thing. I was a grown ass man and I didn't have but one mother. Once I made Candie my wife, then I would kick back and live the life that she expected, but until then, it was whatever.

Once I was processed out, I was led out the doors and to the front lobby of the jail. I looked around for a moment and didn't see Candie. It took a few minutes for me to receive my property, then I walked outside to see if maybe she was out there. Once I stepped outside, I looked up and Joy was walking in my direction. My heart dropped because now I was sure that there was about to be some shit going on. Candie hadn't shown up to court, and she hadn't even bailed me out. Now standing here seeing Joy in front of me, belly protruding and shit ,had me ready to go back to that cell because I had a feeling deep in my gut that some bullshit was in the air.

"What you doing up here, girl?" I said, trying to play it cool as to not hurt Joy's feelings. I mean, shit, she had helped when I was getting arrested, came to court and bailed me out, even though I hadn't asked her for that shit.

Joy smiled and rubbed her belly, and I swear I saw my life flash before my eyes. "Hey, boo, well as soon as I left court I went down to the bail bonds and had everything processed. I knew that you weren't trying to be sitting in that bitch for Christmas," she said sweetly.

I nodded my head. "Good looking," I said, rubbing her stomach and then following her to the car.

I shook my head because she had even driven my car up here. Man, I was most definitely a dead nigga walking.

Chapter 9: Candie

I paced the floor of Sincere's living room while he and Taylor watched me like I was a madwoman, which was understandable considering that I was fresh off of a 7-day tour and I was burning a hole in their carpet with a gun hanging down at my side. I was pissed. No, I was beyond pissed. I was fucking furious, I knew that something was brewing, but having a hunch about some shit and actually knowing some shit was two different things, and most definitely two different feelings.

"Sis, you need to calm down and put that fucking gun away. You act like the nigga in here, and even if he was, I wouldn't let you shoot his ass," Sin said, standing up and walking towards me.

"Sin, sit your ass back down! The fuck you mean you wouldn't let me shoot him? Whose side are you on?" I asked, looking at him like he had sprouted two heads.

Taylor stood up. "He didn't mean it like that, Candie, you know that we're on your side, but you can't go to jail behind his cheating ass. I'm all for fucking him up, but we can't kill his ass," Taylor said.

She was right. I nodded my head and flopped down on the couch. "You're right, Tay, okay it's good."

I looked at my watch. It was getting late and I still had to hit the grocery store to get everything together for Christmas dinner. Honey and the rest of the girls were going to help me cook, and it would be a good distraction from all of the bullshit.

As soon as I got back in Oakland, I had Jamie take me straight to the courthouse. Once we got there and found out what courtroom he would be in, I ran into little miss light bright. This time I was the one to approach her, being that this was now our third encounter. As soon as I walked up to her she held this smug expression like she just knew some shit that I didn't know. I had asked her about Caine and she informed me that she had been fucking with him for almost a year and was carrying his child. Once I heard that, I left the bitch standing right there and walked smooth out of the courthouse. Luckily, Jamie was driving because I would have done a thousand all the way to the house. Shit, I was hot, and Jamie's ass didn't make shit any better because she was talking shit the whole way about how I should have smacked the bitch and what she would do if Caine was her nigga. I was glad once I got to my car because I needed to think, and I didn't want to hear nobody's voice but my own. I rubbed my hands over my face as I sat there on Sin's couch. I hadn't shed one tear and I didn't plan to either. I wouldn't give a damn if Caine's ass never came home, he could go with that bitch because he would be one sorry mothafucka' if he came home to me. I had plans to make him regret the day he ever met me, and definitely the day he ever played me. I put the safety on my gun and dropped it into my purse; I shook my head and laughed because I was on one and tripping. I had too much going for myself to be caught up in some bullshit behind some dick, especially short dick. At least if I was going to go crazy it could be over some long dick that had the ability to fuck me crazy, not short dick that clearly was free for all.

I looked up and Sin and Taylor were staring at me with bewildered expressions on their faces. "My bad, y'all. Tay, can you go with me to the grocery store? Sin, do you mind if we make this a girl's night?" I asked as I came up with the idea to steal all the girls for the night.

I didn't want to be alone because I didn't trust myself to not kill anybody tonight. I was sure that Caine would be released or bailed out, and once he came home I couldn't be accountable for my actions.

"It's all good, sis, you can keep her if you want," Sin said and we all laughed.

"Hey, don't tempt me, Sin. Baby is smart, can cook, and she got a phatty. I might just take yo' bitch," I said, feeling a little better.

Taylor and I grabbed our things and then made our way outside. I sent a group text to Honey, Dezi and Cass and told them to meet me at my house in an hour and to bring some liquor and their presents and wrapping paper. I was going to need a gallon of some good shit to make me feel better, and who better to get shit faced with than my best bitches?

Taylor and I hit the grocery store and it felt like we were in there forever. I hated to go grocery shopping, but I loved to eat. I had sent Caine my grocery list the day I left, and expected to come home and everything would be there, but it wasn't, so now I had to tackle that by myself, well with Taylor. I really liked Tay. She was a great person and I wouldn't mind her being the mother of my brother's child and wife.

"Tay, when do you think you and Sin will be ready to give me a couple of nieces and nephews?" I said as I loaded the cart with boxes of elbow macaroni.

"Damn, a couple? Can I push one out first before you try and stretch my vagina for me?"

I laughed because I had jumped the gun slightly.

"Nah, but really, I know Sincere has baby fever, so I wouldn't mind starting our family next year, but I don't want to just be his baby mama. I'm not a fan of broken families and raising children out of wedlock, and Sin knows that, so if he is ready to step up and make me an honest woman then I'm with that because I'm definitely worth it."

I nodded my head and smiled at Taylor's confidence. She knows what she wants and what she deserves, and she wasn't going to settle for anything less. I needed to soak up some of that attitude when it comes to my own life.

After about two hours, we had finally gotten everything and were on our way to my house. The other ladies were already there. Honey had a spare key to my house, so I was pretty sure they were inside blowing it down and sipping. When I walked through the front door, I could hear Dezi's loud ass mouth coming from the kitchen. Lacey was sitting Indian style on my living room floor with a deck of Uno cards in front of her and some wrapped gifts as well as unwrapped gifts surrounding her. I laughed because she was the type that loved to have game night, she was super competitive, but cool as shit. I spoke to everybody as Taylor and I unloaded the car and brought the groceries into the kitchen

Honey and Cass unpacked the bags as we brought them in. After all of the groceries were handled, we all gathered in the living room with a bottle, some shot glasses and sat down and wrapped presents. After about two hours, we were finally finished wrapping so we gathered around for a couple of rounds of Uno.

"Sis, I know you didn't just invite us all over here for nothing, so what's good?" Honey asked as she threw out a Draw Four for Dezi.

I took the shot in front of me and then looked at everybody. These were my bitches and I loved them to death, but I had to start living life for me because I hadn't been happy in a while and I deserved my happy.

"Well, I have been thinking about moving to L.A. that's where the label is, and I figured that it would be easier to just relocate so that I don't have to fly out there every other week," I said as I reshuffled the deck and dealt out the cards.

"Bitch, that's bullshit and you should know it. What the fuck did that bitch ass nigga do now?" Dezi said, raising her voice a little.

I shook my head, trying not to get pissed all over again but I couldn't help it. I could feel the rage building up in my heart. "What didn't he do? I go up to the damn courthouse and the same little light bright ass bitch that I keep running into is up there belly big and hella shit. So I rock up on the bitch and ask her what's up and she tells me that she's been fucking with Caine and pregnant with his baby. After that, I cut. So let her do that jail shit and bail him out." I looked through my hand and laid out a card.

"Oh hell no, bitch, and we sitting here playing Uno! You should have told us to throw on our hoodies and boots because it's ass whooping season. Where the fuck that nigga at? Matter of fact, hold on!" Dezi jumped up and grabbed her phone. We all sat there staring at her crazy ass as she put the phone to her ear. "Laz! So you knew that your bitch ass patna got a baby on the way?" I shook my head laughing because she was so extra, I could hear Laz yelling through the phone, but I couldn't make out what he was saying.

Dezi sat listening on the phone for a second with an angry look on her face. "Well, you better find his ass before I do because yo' nigga got it coming, doing my sister like this!" She yelled into the phone before hanging up.

This situation was for sure going from bad to worse. I poured another round of shots and took mine as I sat back staring at the ceiling, thinking about my next move. The rest of the night was spent getting drunk and talking shit. Being in the company of my girls helped, but it didn't stop the evil thoughts or the breaking of my heart. I looked online and saw that Caine was no longer in custody and that pissed me off even more when he never came home. I wanted to call Josh and see if he was over there, but I knew that if he said no then I would be ready to tear some shit up.

After a while everybody had passed out on me and I was just up in my feelings. I sent a text to Mal and he responded almost immediately. He asked if he could come and see me and I told him yes. I was drunk and working with feelings, so I didn't give a fuck about anything right now. It was apparent that Caine wasn't coming home and I needed to release some frustration. I know that two wrongs don't make a right, and I was definitely playing with fire letting my ex nigga come and pick me up from the house I shared with my current boyfriend. Mal's ass was crazy and when he got into his moods he could easily pop up and cause some very unnecessary drama, but for the moment, I just felt like fuck it all. I crept to the bathroom and hopped into the shower in an attempt to sober me up a little, but I was too gone for that. After I had washed up, I threw on some thot gear; leggings with no panties and a hoodie with no shirt or bra with a pair of Uggs and waited for Mal to hit me.

After I dressed, Mal called and let me know that he was pulling up. I grabbed my phone and keys and walked out the front door. I had to stand there for a second, my head was spinning and I knew I couldn't walk in a straight line. I laughed to myself as I watched

Mal's headlights come up the street and stop at the curb, I stood there on the porch and smiled to myself. I didn't have an ounce of guilt. It felt good being back around Mal after so long. Everything had been good lately, but I knew that the good would only last for so long because soon as Mal didn't get his way it would be fonk season and I wasn't ready for that.

Malcolm hopped out of his car and walked up to my porch, he looked around for a minute checking his surroundings before he placed his arms around my waist and leaned in for a kiss. "Damn, you drank up the bar?" he said as he picked me up and stared into my face under the light from the porch.

I giggled as I felt his facial hair tickle my chin, damn my drunk ass was about to cause some shit. I was sure if he reached between my legs his hand would come back soaking wet, being next to him always did that to me. Mal set me back down on my feet and grabbed my hand as we walked to his whip. Once we were inside sitting in the plush seats, I looked over at Mal and he was just staring at me.

"Damn, what I got shit on my face?" I said as he just smiled at me.

"Nah, never that, you know you too saucy to ever be sitting like that. Real shit, my nigga, I miss you and I sometimes think that I need you back in my life, full time."

I shook my head because I couldn't front and act like I didn't have those thoughts and feelings sometimes too. My love for Mal was real, so it would never just go away, but it did take a back burner to the love that I now had for Caine.

Mal and I were young when we were together. We were also super reckless, but if I was rocking he was most definitely rolling and vice versa. That was the difference between him and Caine. When we were together we moved in sync. When I was pushing he was pushing with me and I really felt as if he supported me in everything that I did. With Caine, I feel like he only supports me when it benefits him too, and that's not how it should be. If we're together then we move together, we push each other and some more shit. I leaned my seat back and threw my arms behind my head as Mal leaned over and stuck his hand under my hoodie.

"Damn, your little nasty ass ain't got on no bra, do you have panties on, freak?" he said with an amused expression on his face.

I winked at him and shook my head no. "Damn, baby, you trying to get kidnapped," Mal said as he adjusted his pants.

I kicked back and let him fondle me as he drove up into the hills and found a place to park facing the Oakland skyline. Malcolm grabbed my hand and pulled me toward him. "Come here," he said as I pushed his seat back to make room between him and the steering wheel.

I climbed over and straddled his lap. I could feel his stiffness up against the crotch of my leggings. My body shuddered as he scooted me forward and my pussy rubbed against the length of his penis.

"Shit," I said as I tried to keep myself from just bouncing smooth on his shit.

For an hour, Mal and I just talked and flirted back and forth. I was all over him and he was all over me. The shit was just equal, it wasn't one sided and it felt good to feel genuine love and attraction. I didn't get that from Caine. He didn't say ,'babe you're beautiful,' or 'you look nice today,' he didn't offer to listen to my new music or sit and write with me anymore. Yeah, sometimes we did have our moments every blue moon, but there was no consistency. But I knew better than to think that the grass would be greener with Mal. Tonight I was just having fun. I leaned in and kissed Malcolm softly on his lips.

"More," he said, and I did it again.

Mal pulled my leggings down and released his manhood in one swift motion. "You an expert at fucking bitches in cars?" I asked as I lifted my legs so that he could pull my leggings off.

"Nah, just you," he said as he slid me down until he was filling up my insides.

I couldn't even respond to that comment; I was feeling so good. Mal and I fucked until the sun came up right there in his car in the hills. I shook my head because that was some young shit. I sat back in my seat and grabbed the wipes out of the glove box and tried to clean up before I put my clothes back on.

Once we pulled back up in front of my house I instantly felt bad. I was mad at Caine for stepping outside of our relationship and cheating on me with other bitches, and I had let my anger and liquor take over and lead me right onto the lap of another nigga, and a nigga that I had feelings for at that. It could never just be casual sex when you had feelings for somebody, it just didn't work like that.

I looked over at Mal and his eyes were low as he flashed me a half smile. "I ain't fucking with you, Mal," I said as I grabbed my keys and phone and reached for the door.

"But you need to be. I'll hit you later when I wake up, and keep that lame nigga out my pussy, C," He said as I stepped out of the passenger seat and stood on the sidewalk. I shook my head and smiled. "I'm serious, Candie Monroe, quit fucking with that lame nigga and come back home."

I tilted my head and twisted my lips as I stared at him through the car window. If only it was that easy. I waved to Mal then turned around and walked in the house. It was after 7 A.M. and I was praying that everybody was still sleep.

Cass was standing in the kitchen sipping a cup of coffee and looking in her phone, she was always the early bird. "Don't let the actions of a fool turn you into a fool too," she said, never looking up.

I nodded my head and grabbed a bottle of water out of the refrigerator and walked out of the kitchen and into my room. I heard Cass loud and clear and she was right, I couldn't stoop to his level and play tit for tat. We were grown, and if we couldn't get it together then this is where it needed to end. All of this creeping shit wasn't me and I didn't want to let Caine's infidelity turn me into somebody that I couldn't stand to face.

***

I was running around the house like a chicken with my head cut off, trying to make sure that I had everything together. It was Christmas day, and all of the food was finished, the gifts were under the tree and wrapped so beautifully, now I was just waiting for everybody to arrive. My dad would be coming later on with his girlfriend or what my siblings and I liked to call his flavor of the month. I had stayed up all night getting the dinner prepared, with the help of Cass, Taylor and Dezi. Taylor had put her foot in the gumbo, and Cass and Dezi had helped me with the ham, macaroni and cheese, greens, roast and desserts.

Caine had been staying at Josh's house, scared to death to come home. I had talked to him once since he had gotten bailed out, but he couldn't answer not one question that I asked, so I advised him that it was in his best interest to stay the fuck from around me until he found the balls to come clean. I waited for two days for him to text or call and tell me the truth, and all he keeps saying is just let him come home and talk, and that was not happening. It was going on three in the afternoon and I had told everybody that they should arrive around four, so I needed to get upstairs to get dressed. I don't know why us black folk always feel the need to get all dolled up on the holidays where we are about to sit around family and friends and stuff our faces all damn night, but I had bought something real cute to wear anyway.

I turned the stove on low so that the food would stay warm, and went to get dressed, I checked my phone and I had a text from Mal and a message from Cree saying Merry Christmas and both letting me know that they had gotten me a gift. I smiled at the gesture because I didn't expect anything from either one of them. I had even gotten a gift from my label, so I was all smiles this Christmas, even with all of the bullshit going on between Caine and I.

Around 4:30, everybody started to arrive and my house was popping with chatter. I had turned on some Christmas music and not those boring ass Christmas carols, but some black folk Christmas songs. I had gone online last night and downloaded Christmas songs from all of my favorite artists and made a play list to play throughout the evening. I moved around the kitchen and made sure that all of the food was out and accessible, I refused to make plates. Everybody could come and eat whenever they wanted. We weren't a traditional family and didn't need to eat all together like we were. Once everybody had arrived, we blessed the food as a group and continued to chill. My dad had come in with a large bottle of Hennessy and some thick ass lady who looked like she had two basketballs in her jeans. My father had moved to Atlanta about three years ago and he loved it out there, and I was sure he did, especially since damn near all the bitches were walking around with fat asses like that.

I was standing in the kitchen talking with Lacey and Dezi when Jamie walked in with a crazy look on her face. She walked over to me and pulled me to the side handing me her phone. I looked at the screen and it was pictures of Caine and that high yellow bitch, Joy. I looked closer and realized that I was looking at professional pregnancy pictures. I instantly felt rage. This nigga couldn't even keep it real and he had gone and taken pictures with this hoe, like did he think that I wouldn't see the damn pictures or something? I stared at the pictures for a moment and tried to calm myself down, but it was impossible.

"Joshua!" I yelled from the hallway.

After a couple of seconds, Josh was standing in front of me with a worried look on his face. I never called him by his full name, so I know that he knew something was up. "Call yo' brother and tell him to get his bitch ass here now!" I said shoving the phone in his hand so that he could see the seriousness of the situation. I know it was Christmas but these were all my closest family and friends so I couldn't care less what anybody thought about how I was about to go in on Caine's ass.

I walked away from Josh and Jamie and grabbed large trash bags out of the kitchen. I went into my bedroom and started pulling out drawers and emptying all of Caine's clothing into the bags. I grabbed shoebox after shoebox and threw them into bags too. Once I was satisfied that I had bagged all of Caine's belongings, I had Honey and Dezi help me drag the bags out past the front yard and into the middle of the street.

"Candie, cut this shit out now!" My dad yelled as I walked past him to grab another bag.

"Dad, with all due respect, leave me alone and let me handle this shit like I please." I turned and looked at everybody as they sat around looking at me like I was crazy. "If anybody has an issue then you are more than welcomed to pack you a plate, grab your gift, and get the fuck out," I said calmly.

I didn't mean to disrespect anybody, but the state of mind I was in had me on some other shit. Caine had fucked up royally and he had picked the wrong day to let this shit hit the fan. Holiday or not, he was about to feel me. I looked around and nobody moved.

Once I had all of Caine's belongings on the street, I went into the trunk of Caine's old school Cutlass that sat in the driveway and grabbed the gas can that he kept inside. I doused all of the bags and pulled a shirt from one of the bags that I lit on fire with a lighter. When it began to burn, I threw it on top of the pile and waited for it to catch. As the pile started to burn, I heard tires hit the corner. I looked up and saw Caine's car coming to a stop and another car right behind it. I stood there breathing hard with my hands on my hips as Caine hopped out angrily. He ran up to me yelling and I was so zoned out that I could barely hear what he was saying.

I could feel Caine shaking me, but now I was looking past him and wondering why his pregnant bitch was standing in front of my house like she belonged there. I was so mad that I felt like I was floating. It all felt like a movie that I was sitting back watching. I took a step back and watched as Caine turned toward Jamie and slapped the shit out of her. I just stood and stared at the exchange between the two of them, trying to put all of my thoughts together.

"I'm pregnant too! This is how you do me?"

My eyes bucked open as it dawned on me that those words were coming from Jamie's mouth. I shook my head as I realized that the people I loved and trusted whole-heartedly had betrayed me. I looked behind me and saw all of my family and friends just standing there staring, and I couldn't believe that they were standing here witnessing my greatest heartbreak. I reached into the small of my back and pulled my gun and released the safety.

"Candie! No!" I could hear my dad and brother yelling, but my hand had a mind of its own.

I heard the gunshots, I heard the sirens, but I don't remember the faces or anything that I was looking at before I pulled the trigger. I could feel the sting of hot tears flow down my face, and then I felt jolts of pain all through my body. It was like my body was on fire and then everything went black.

Chapter 10: Caine

I sat down in the middle of the hospital waiting room with my head in my hands. I had tears and snot all over my face and I didn't have the strength to clean it up. I felt people all around me, but it was silent. I couldn't look up. I was lost; I had done so much trying to live my life how I wanted to, that I didn't take into account that my actions would bring about greater consequences than I was prepared to be accountable for. I had played my girl like a fool time and time again with the mindset that I would settle down one day and get it together when I was ready. I had moved so reckless, fathering two children outside of my relationship, one being with somebody close to Candie. In turn, Candie had snapped and shot all of us. The bullet that had hit me went in one leg and out the other, but Jamie and Joy weren't as lucky. Their wounds were fatal and they were both pronounced dead at the scene. The police had come almost immediately after the shots rang out.

They had commanded Candie over and over again to lower her gun and surrender, but she just wouldn't do it. She continued to shake her head and tell them they would just have to kill her because she wasn't dropping shit. After twenty minutes of trying to persuade Candie to surrender, she took a shot toward the officers as they attempted to get Jamie's body off the scene, and she was gunned down by the police right where she stood. I was hurt and lost beyond words; my actions had turned this Christmas into a massacre. My actions had caused three innocent women to lose their lives tonight. How does somebody recover from that? I had lost the love of my life and both of my unborn children and their mothers in a matter of minutes. My mother always told me to watch how I treated women because every action came with an equal or greater reaction.

I would have to live with this forever. No matter what I did and where I went, I knew that this would haunt me for the rest of my life. The blood of five lives was on my hands. I had left Joy's young son motherless due to my selfish ass ways. I looked up and I couldn't bring myself to even look at Candie's family. I knew that they blamed me and would never forgive me. Honey had already jumped on me twice since they took Candie's body away, and I couldn't fight her or blame her because at the moment I wanted to die myself.

"Young man, I really want to strangle you to death, but I have been young before and I know that sometimes the allure of temptation doesn't seem like shit. But I hope and pray that you have learned something from all of this. As much as I hate you at this very moment, I know this day will haunt you forever and that's punishment enough for your ass."

I stared at Candie's father as he walked away and straight out of the hospital doors.

Join our mailing list to get a notification when Leo Sullivan Presents has another release!

Text LEOSULLIVAN to 22828 to join!

To submit a manuscript for our review, email us at leosullivanpresents@gmail.com

Coming Soon from Sullivan Productions!

BAD *Boys* AIN'T NO GOOD,
Good Boys Ain't No'
FUN

QUISHA DYNAE

CPSIA information can be obtained
at www.ICGtesting.com
Printed in the USA
LVOW13s1756091217
559234LV00027B/248/P